D0436479

feathered

ALSO BY LAURA KASISCHKE

Boy Heaven

feathered

LAURA KASISCHKE

HARPER TEEN
An Imprint of HarperCollins*Publishers*

HarperTeen is an imprint of HarperCollins Publishers.

Feathered

www.harperteen.com

Library of Congress Cataloging-in-Publication Data
Kasischke, Laura, date.
Feathered / Laura Kasischke.—1st ed.
p. cm.
Summary: While on spring break in Cancún, Mexico, high-school seniors and best friends Anne and Michelle accept the wrong ride and Michelle is lost—seemingly forever.
ISBN 978-0-06-081317-8 (trade bdg.)
ISBN 978-0-06-081318-5 (lib. bdg.)
[1. Spring break—Fiction. 2. Best friends—Fiction. 3. Friendship—Fiction. 4. Missing persons—Fiction. 5. Coming of age—Fiction. 6. Cancún (Mexico)—Fiction. 7. Mexico—Fiction.] I. Title.
PZ7.K1178Fea 2008 2007006993
[Fic]—dc22 CIP
AC

Typography by Joel Tippie
1 2 3 4 5 6 7 8 9 10

First Edition

For Bill

In former times, the soul was feathered all over.

Plato

She saw the myriad gods, and beyond God his own ineffable eternity; she saw that there were ranges of life beyond our present life, ranges of mind beyond our present mind. . . .

Sri Aurobindo

one

one

Michelle

Oh, he is not a human. He is a god. His feathers rustle around her as he takes her by the shoulders—but his skin is also the skin of a snake. Cool, daggered, iridescent. When the knife is raised, she isn't afraid. She does not close her eyes. After the first plunge into her chest, she feels nothing more. Not fear. Not sadness. After the next, he reaches in, and what he pulls out is the most luminous blue-green bird she has ever seen. It is newborn, but it has always been alive, and he lets it fly from his hand into the sky. She watches it crashing into the blue, singing beautiful notes, a few of its green feathers falling from its wings, settling quietly around her.

two

Anne

AFTERWARD, TERRI WILL tell everyone back at school that, from the beginning, she knew something terrible was going to happen on spring break.

She'll say she knew it already on the plane as we passed over that long black nothingness between the Midwest and Mexico. She'll say she looked down and saw headlights creeping along some highway in Nebraska, or Oklahoma, and had a cold, dead feeling.

Something *bad* was going to happen.

She *knew.*

Maybe even back in February, when we'd booked the trip. She'll say she almost told us back then, but hadn't wanted to ruin spring break for us, if, you know, her feeling turned out to be nothing.

"She's so full of shit," they'll say back at school behind her back. "She's about as psychic as my ass."

And, in truth, Terri was the one who'd nixed the cruise we'd considered taking (*"I get seasick"*) and sold us on Cancún.

Well, Terri, and MTV, and a brochure with a picture of the Hotel del Sol on it.

Sun!

Sand!

Tiki bar on the beach!

Poolside happy hour!

Peaceful days, wild nights!

I'd had, myself, no premonitions. No omens. Nothing. I was, on that plane to Mexico, not even really thinking. I had a string bikini on under my sweater and jeans, and a list of the drinks I wanted to try at that tiki bar. *Kahlua & Cream. Blue Margaritas. "The Bull" (tequila, beer, and lemonade). The Pineapple Leap. The Mexicol. The Furnace. The Cockroach. The Submarine.*

It was the end of senior year.

The drinking age in Mexico was eighteen.

The tests and the applications were finally over.

I'd gotten into the best of the colleges to which I'd applied.

My parents had bought the plane ticket for me, and given me a thousand dollars to blow, as a reward for making the honor roll every year since seventh grade. I had the center seat, my two best friends on either side of me, and a week ahead of me in which to be a completely different girl than I was at home. If Terri was having premonitions or second thoughts, I wouldn't have wanted to know anyway. I was happy, excited, full of flimsy plans:

The boys I'd meet. The drinks. The tan.

The way you think you're making plans for the future, when, really, it's making plans for *you.*

Well, of course, I didn't know that then, but now I do.

three

Michelle

OUTSIDE THE LITTLE plastic window on the plane between Illinois and Mexico, it's just black. It's nothing. When Michelle Tompkins puts her hand to it she can feel it—all that nothing blowing around out there, holding her up.

But it feels secure, too, that little window. Smudged and simple. And this plane full of strangers and her two friends seems still and peaceful in the sky.

Michelle has never been afraid to fly. Every summer she's gone to Oregon with her mother. Twice they've flown to Florida to visit her grandparents. During one of those trips, an emergency landing had to be made because of a malfunction with the plane's navigational system. Once there was so much turbulence that the overhead compartments snapped open and luggage spilled out into the aisles. But it didn't faze Michelle. She'd felt then, as she does now, safe in the sky. In fact, she wishes it felt *more* like flying. To her, on a plane, it doesn't even feel as if they're in the air at all. It seems as if they're simply in the backseat of her mother's Saab, like when they were little girls being carpooled to and from day care—back there together pretending, maybe, to be on a plane.

What did the pilot say?

Thirty thousand feet?

Occasionally she can see what looks like headlights, or searchlights, moving around in the vastness down there. She tries to watch the lights until they disappear, and then to force herself to believe that there's another person down there and that, someday, she might brush elbows with that person at a train station or a video store, and they'll never know, never even be able to guess, that they have this connection.

But it's impossible.

She might believe in *them*, but how can they

believe in *her*? Who on that earth could guess that, overhead, there is an eighteen-year-old girl on spring break flying to a foreign country for the first time in her life, looking down?

What does she want on spring break?

She wants to laugh hard at her friends' jokes. She wants to drink tequila—not so much that she's really drunk, but enough that she's spinning and giddy. She wants to forget about Illinois, and the deep strange loneliness she feels every time she realizes that she's graduating in two months, and that she will be going away to a college on the opposite side of the country from the one where Anne will be, and where her mother is. She wants a whole week of not seeing the look in her mother's eyes when she passes her bedroom—that *I'm-being-brave-although-knowing-you'll-be-leaving-is-killing-me* expression, so full of raw grief and longing that Michelle has, at least twice already (and it's not even summer vacation yet!) had to bury her head in her pillow so her mother wouldn't hear her cry herself to sleep.

She's never been on a real trip without her mother before. Oh, a week at Anne's parents' cottage up north. Two weeks at Camp Daggett. But never on a plane without her. Never another country.

She wants to know that she can do it. And for her mother to know she can do it. She's eighteen, after all.

She wants to wear her tankini on the beach. Flirt with a boy who's never even been to Illinois, let alone been a student at Glendale High. She wants to forget about Glendale High, and the boys there—almost all of whom she's known since kindergarten. Or before that. Little Friends Day Care.

She wants to swim in the ocean. Get a tan. Celebrate everything that's almost over so that she can get on with everything that's almost next. Before the tickets had even been paid for, Michelle imagined spring break *over*—and the photograph she'd tack to her bulletin board:

There she is—another American girl in a foreign place for her spring break, arms tossed over the shoulders of her friends, the three of them turned toward her camera and a stranger (who has graciously offered to snap the image for them) as an expression of radiant joy flashes across her face at the moment the picture is taken.

Of course, she's had these premonitions before. How exciting high school would be—and then it turned out to be like middle school with more stress. Or prom, only to have Scott Moore leave her sitting at a table in the cafeteria by herself while he drove off in search of a bottle of whiskey to smuggle in. Or the countless other special events—homecomings, field trips, dates—which were supposed to be the landmarks of a teenage girl's life, and which paled in comparison to most Sunday afternoons spent watching old movies on TV in the living room with her mom.

Either she never *learned,* or experience had not managed to squeeze the hope and excitement out of her.

It didn't matter.

She was full of radiant expectations, and it didn't matter to her at all that from where she sat looking down at the earth from the window of that plane, the darkness spreading out behind her and the darkness spread out ahead of her looked very much the same.

four
Anne

MICHELLE TOMPKINS WAS my best friend. My oldest friend. My first. How could I have made any friends before her? We'd met in day care when we were three years old.

Truly, we hadn't ever even really *met.*

Like my mother, or my grandmother, or the idea of juice and the postal service and green grass, Michelle Tompkins was always just *there,* from the very beginning—a small girl in a blue dress in the corner of my eye. The two of us were standing in line with many other very small children, waiting to have our pictures taken, and every one of us was wearing a little sticker badge that said I'M #1! From somewhere behind us a scratchy tape played a song I loved:

I had a little nut tree, nothing could it bear, but a silver nutmeg, and a golden pear . . .

Michelle's ponytail was secured with a blue scrunchy that matched her dress.

I looked at her badge and, although I couldn't read yet, I knew what it meant, and I thought to myself, *This little girl is #1.*

I'd forgotten, somehow, that I too was wearing a sticker that said I'M #1! It wouldn't have mattered at that moment though, because Michelle seemed, clearly to me, to be the first, best girl.

We didn't know it yet, but we had a lot in common. Mothers who worked and worried too much. Bad habits—nail-biting, hair-twirling. We both lived on busy streets and weren't allowed to play in our front yards because our mothers thought we could be kidnapped, or that some teenage boy might jump the curb, speeding in his car with bad brakes, and run us over on our own stoops.

The other kids got cookies in plastic sandwich bags for their snacks. We got carrot sticks, pomegranate seeds, or lightly salted *edamame.* We loved cats. Michelle and her mother had four of them. My father was allergic, so my mother collected cat pillows, cat magnets.

But, unlike me, Michelle had no father.

"My father was a sperm," she'd say. "My mother picked him because he had blue-green eyes and was a cello player. He cost a thousand bucks. Quite a bargain, huh?"

Here, she'd open her arms wide, to indicate herself—*Voilà!*—as if she were some nerdy kid's successful science fair experiment.

But she would tell you seriously, too, that if you ever decided to have a kid by choosing your own sperm from a catalog at a sperm bank, it would be better if you weren't as open with your kid about it as Michelle's mother had been with her.

"You can never shake it," she said. "Every man you see, you think, *maybe that's my sperm.* I mean, *father.* It's like the whole world's full of sperms, walking around, crossing the street, buying burgers at McDonald's. She should have told me that she'd had a one-night stand, and he was dead."

But Michelle's mother had a policy of being open about *everything.*

She'd talk and talk about things she thought kids

should be talked to about until there was nothing left to say on any subject. Nothing left to the imagination at all. Menstruation. Oral sex. Drugs. Body image. Personal hygiene.

And, because she was a speech therapist, her enunciation when she talked about these things was so crisp it was as if every consonant that came out of her mouth were made of steel. You couldn't pretend you hadn't heard what she'd said—even when, over gyros at George's Coney Island, you desperately hoped she hadn't just said the word *clitoris.*

"Good morning, girls," she'd say when she dropped Michelle off at school, depositing her from the backseat of her Saab into our circle of friends at Earhart Elementary, or Weintraub Middle, or, finally, Glendale High.

"Good morning, Ms. Tompkins," we'd say.

"You know to call me Roberta," she'd tell us, but we never could.

Roberta Tompkins looked like Janis Joplin might have looked if she'd gotten her act together. Gotten a teaching certificate. Moved to a suburb. Lived to be fifty. Become a single mother. She wore a lot of purple, and fat beads from Guatemala. Sweaters from Peru—sweaters so heavy that just to look at them would make you itch. She was attractive enough, but so solid and blunt that you could sort of see why it was easier for her to make a baby with a sperm, and a syringe, than with a man, in a bed.

Because *this* was Michelle's mother, it seemed that Michelle's sperm must have been the quiet, circumspect type, because Michelle was mostly both of these things. And he must have been small, because, unlike her mother, Michelle was delicate. Not just thin—her bones, it seemed, were *flutey*. Her skeleton seemed to be made as much of air and marrow as the more solid stuff of bone. Most of my bracelets could wrap around her wrist two times, and still there'd be some slack. She sang, and Mr. Brecht, the choir director, hauled her out for every special occasion and set her in front of the student body or the parents gathered in the auditorium, for a solo.

When she sang, Michelle grew taller, like a candle flame surging upward when a window opens. A soprano, her high notes were so clear and bright you had to squint when she hit them. Her high notes would slap the smirks off even the most cynical boys in the school. Babies would stop crying. Mothers would shed tears.

But when the music stopped, she was just Michelle Tompkins again. Pretty enough, but not a girl boys turned around to watch wiggle down the hall. She'd had a couple of boyfriends, but they'd all broken up with her (gently) when flashier girls came along. Usually Michelle just accepted this gracefully—two days of silence followed by one day of sighing and pushing her lunch away from her at the table in the cafeteria, and then she was just Michelle again.

Only Dave Ebert broke her heart.

He was a tenor in the choir, and we'd all told her we thought he was gay before they started dating. ("His fingernails," Terri said, "are the dead giveaway. He polishes them, Michelle.") When he dumped her for Barb Schmidt after Christmas vacation we all told Michelle it was because he was trying to cover up the fact that he was gay by going out with the girl with the biggest boobs in the school.

But it was two weeks before I heard Michelle laugh out loud again, and even after that, the quiet trailed around her like a gown for months.

"We're going to get you a new guy in Cancún,"

I'd said. "A college guy." Michelle had seemed happy about it. She'd bought a silver metallic tankini with her waitressing money. It made her breasts look bigger, we both agreed. I'd given her a pair of beaded sandals with three-inch heels that were too small for me. In that suit, wearing those sandals, Michelle looked like an entirely different girl from the one who sang in the choir at Glendale High. She was ready to be a different girl, to be with a different kind of boy, at least for the week.

"This is going to be the party that starts our new lives," I'd said, and Michelle had agreed—although we'd also both agreed that we wouldn't *just* party. We'd see the sights. We'd snorkel. We'd bring some books to the beach.

Michelle's mother had made us read up on the Yucatán Peninsula after we booked the plane tickets and hotel. She said it was shameful, going to a place like that with such a rich history, and not appreciating it. It was so typically *American*—overrunning and ruining these idyllic places without knowing anything about them. Michelle's mother had been in the Peace Corps. For her own spring break, her senior year in high school, she'd gone to Appalachia to help build houses and dig wells.

At first, we were blasé about it (Michelle's mother's lectures had a way of turning us blasé about things we might otherwise have cared about), but then she got our attention with a picture she downloaded off the internet:

That pyramid—temple, ziggurat, whatever you would call it. Two thousand years old. All that massive, ascending, white stone under a pale blue sky.

At the top of it, the article said, they used to slash the throats of their sacrifices, then open up their chests and pull out their beating hearts, hold them up to their god—Quetzalcoatl, a hideous feathered serpent who lived on human flesh—until the steps ran red with blood.

Apparently at the center of the pyramid there was an altar on which they burned the victims' hearts. You could squeeze through a passageway and see it.

"Wow," we'd said, leaning over Michelle's mother's shoulder, peering into her computer screen.

"It's called the Castle of the Plumed Serpent," she said, tapping the picture. And, even on a computer screen, photographed, miniaturized, made of nothing but pixels and light, those ruins looked enormous and mysterious and beautiful—a place on earth you might step into and find yourself in another world.

"Awesome," we both said—the word we used and loved so much, a word that could be applied as easily to a two-thousand-year-old pyramid, in a jungle, where an ancient civilization had sacrificed virgins, as to a nice pink shade of lipgloss. But, in this case, what Michelle's mother was showing us really *was* awesome.

"Yes," she said. "It *is* awesome, girls. Life isn't all about swimming pools and nightclubs. If you're willing to be awed, there are awesome things in this world."

five

Michelle

WHEN MICHELLE'S MOTHER had dropped the three girls off at the airport, it was sleeting. But, before they'd left the house, they'd checked The Weather Channel. In Cancún, it said, the temperature was ninety-two degrees, and they had to think hard about what to wear for a car trip through sleet and slush, thirty-two degrees—the low, stone, cold gray of March in Illinois, and the old Saab's heater only a vague rattling attempt at warmth—ending in that tropical heat.

Sitting on the couch, listening to the sleet tick against the windows, waiting for Michelle's mother to say it was time to go, it seemed impossible that somewhere there were balmy breezes, colorful birds in leafy trees, a blue sky, the smell of ocean in the air, and that they could possibly travel to it in an evening. That they could step out of a plane in five hours and find themselves wrapped in it.

So, they decided to layer.

Michelle put on a tank top under a thin white sweater, tights under her short khaki skirt. Terri put on a pale green sleeveless cotton dress, and a black sweater. Black tights, too. Anne had on a string bikini beneath her sweatshirt and jeans. In the Saab they wore their down jackets but shrugged them off when Michelle's mother pulled up to the curb under the sign for their airline. They sprinted as quickly as they could from the curb to the automatic doors, pulling their wheeled luggage behind them while the uniformed baggage handlers, in their heavy coats, hands shoved deep into their pockets, cheered them on. "Spring break! Whoo-hooo!"

But as soon as Michelle got inside, she remembered that she'd forgotten to kiss her mother goodbye. She turned, and looked, and saw her mother still sitting at the curb, waiting behind the wheel of her car, knowing that Michelle would come back.

She did.

This time, as she ran through the winter air it clawed straight through the thin sleeves of her sweater. A slow burn on her arms. She yanked open the door, leaned over the passenger side, and said, "I love you, Mom," and kissed her mother's cheek, which was soft and warm and smelled of her Saab's heater—dust, time, her entire childhood, hundreds and hundreds of gentle miles traveled safely around Glendale, Illinois.

"I love you, too, baby," her mother said. "Be good. Be safe." There was a watery sheen in her eyes.

"Don't worry too much, Mom," Michelle said.

Her mother said, "Let me worry, but you take care of yourself."

"I will," Michelle said, and closed the door between them.

Michelle's mother was not like her friends' mothers. She knew about spring break. What could happen. What *did*. She'd watched the *20/20* show about kids in Daytona. Girls getting drunk, passing out in hot tubs. Oral sex in public places. Alcohol poisoning. Kids falling off balconies. Unlike her friends' mothers,

Michelle's didn't just shrug it off as the behavior of other people's kids. She'd sat down with Michelle and said, "I have to be able to trust you, Shell. It's all I have. My only other option is to lock you up, and eventually you'd get out, and that's no way to live and learn about the world. So, I'm trusting you."

That talk, sitting on the edge of Michelle's bed the week before spring break, surrounded by stuffed animals (what would she do with them when she left for college?), with the light from her window pouring whitely all over the eyelet comforter and the roses on the throw rug on her floor—it was as if her mother had given her a little set of wings. A set of wings she'd sewn over the years for her only daughter—invisible, delicate, intended to attach somewhere behind her back, where she couldn't see them but could use them if she needed them.

It was, Michelle knew, her mother's love for her.

"Right, Shell? I can trust you? Right?"

"Yes, Mom," Michelle had said without any of the usual sarcasm or rolling of her eyes.

She understood what her mother was giving her, and took it.

* * *

Now there is a bit of turbulence, a half second during which Michelle's heart seems to sail out of her before snapping back into place, and then the plane levels, steadies—a slow needle passing through a dense piece of black cloth. Beside her, Anne is doing the crossword puzzle in the in-flight magazine. The flight attendant walks through and picks up the empty trays from their dinners. Michelle looks out at the sky and imagines falling into it. Like a penny tossed into a well—faster and faster as she gets closer to the earth, plummeting toward the surface of a dark lake, or a forest, or a cornfield—except that, at the last minute, she remembers her wings, swoops back up, flies until she's here again, outside this little tin can looking in, and then deciding to fly higher and faster and farther, straight toward the stars.

six

Anne

WE WERE SCHEDULED to land in Mexico at 5 A.M., and, as the jet made its way over the Yucatán Peninsula, we could see dawn inching up on the right side of the plane. Michelle had the window seat. She said, "You should look," tapping the little plastic window.

I did. It looked as if thin, pale-red fingers were reaching up over the side of the world, as if the earth were being held up in a pink hand, as if some goddess had it all cradled in her palm. Above that glowing hand, a few bright stars still twinkled.

"Amazing, huh?" Michelle asked, leaning farther back so I could see it better.

But I closed my eyes and sat straight up again in

my seat. I was done looking. Almost everything outside of that window was more than I wanted to see. I hated flying. When the plane had taken off, I'd gone rigid, as I always did, with panic. That tinny feeling. The way the jet wobbled like a toy before smashing into the air. I'd gripped the armrest so tightly that my knuckles hurt, and squeezed my eyes shut, biting my lower lip with my top teeth. I hated take-offs most of all—those moments before flying when the loose mechanics, and the absurdity of it, were impossible to ignore. We were, obviously, too heavy to fly. Any idiot could see that, that if you tried to heft something enormous into the air, it was going to crash.

Michelle had reached over and put her hand on my arm, and then said something soothing to me under her breath. I couldn't hear it over the roar of the engines and the sound of my heart pounding in my ears, but by then we were flying, and the plane began to level out, and the flight attendants started to move around, smiling blithely, and I'd forgotten for a while that we were in the air. I'd forgotten for *hours*. I'd read the in-flight magazine. I'd managed to fill in all but two rows of the crossword puzzle. I'd read my book. I got up to go to the bathroom, scooching over Terri's knees because she'd fallen asleep. I ate my soggy roast beef croissant and drank two Diet Cokes.

But, suddenly, seeing the land and the ocean under us and the sun coming up, I realized that we were eventually going to have to land, and I gripped the armrest again, gritted my teeth.

"Come on," Michelle said sweetly. She tapped my arm, and when I didn't open my eyes, she just left her hand on top of it. I could feel her watching me. I knew she was amused, that she was waiting for me to open my eyes so she could smile at me, try to jolly me out of my terror. But I couldn't open my eyes, and her smile would only have made me feel worse.

"Anne," she said. "We're not even landing yet. Are you going to stay like this the whole—"

"Shhh," I said. "I don't want to talk."

She said nothing else. I could tell she was looking out the window now, not at me. She knew when to leave me alone. We may have thought of ourselves as soul mates, as sisters, but we knew where each other's boundaries began and ended, too. We each had a mother who couldn't take a step back, and we knew what that was like. Mothers who had to know everything about us, *understand* it—and, if they didn't, had to try to change us into daughters they *could* understand.

My mother, on plane trips like this (once, to Montreal, another time to Portland, Maine, and several trips to Florida to see my grandparents) would not leave me alone. She'd lean over, cooing. And when that didn't work, nudge me with her arm. And then she'd start to argue:

"What are you so afraid of, Anne? You're a hundred and twenty-seven times more likely to die in a car accident on the way to an airport than to die in a plane crash."

When I still would not release my death grip on the armrest, she'd start to threaten me:

"I swear, Anne, I'm never going to take you on another plane if you're going to act like this."

Once, she even tried to pry my fingers off the armrest. It didn't work.

But Michelle knew when to let it go.

She just kept her hand on my arm, and went back to looking out the window. She was willing to let me have my fear.

The plane shuddered.

She patted my hand.

After it steadied again, and I managed to open my eyes, Michelle said, gently, "Maybe you could just look out for one more second? It's pretty amazing, Anne."

I took a deep breath, and did.

She was right.

In the strange light of the sun rising over the horizon, I could see a long expanse of foil blue, swirling with pinks and greens, interrupted by what must have been the Yucatán Peninsula, jutting out like a boot, or a claw.

But then I felt something shut down under us, and the air seemed to part, and I went rigid in my seat again and closed my eyes. Over the intercom, a flight attendant began her instructions. First, in English. (We needed to take our seats. Secure our trays. Fasten our seat belts.) And then in Spanish, which just sounded like musical nonsense to me.

When the flight attendant was done with her instructions, the intercom went dead, and for a weightless moment it seemed as if our plane was headed toward the ground nose first, at an alarming speed. My eyes opened involuntarily, and I gasped loudly enough that Terri turned and gave me her *what-the-fuck?* look.

Then, it felt as if we'd been caught by a gust of wind. Buoyed. Saved. And, despite myself, I looked out the window and saw that the ground, bathed in sunrise, was very close, speeding toward us. I felt the wheels of the plane seem to kick stiffly out of the belly, and then we were roaring along a runway again—but this time, instead of roaring through gray sleet, we were roaring through a blur of green. Trees and shrubs and shadows. When I looked over at Michelle I saw that she was watching me, calmly. There was a crown of light from the overhead reading lamp in her hair. It shone there like a wispy halo. She was smiling, not mocking me—although there was a light film of perspiration over every inch of my body. Michelle was just smiling as if she were happy for me that my ordeal was over. She said, "Now that wasn't so bad, was it? You can fly, after all, Anne."

seven

Michelle

WHEN SHE WAS six years old, Michelle Tompkins was in the backseat of her mother's car on the way to Half Moon Lake. It was summer, and the world outside the car was so green it appeared, also, to be soft, to be swallowing, to be dark. A green cave, despite the high sun in a clear blue sky.

The windows were unrolled, and Michelle could hear birds by the thousands chirping and cawing and shrieking in the branches. The radio was playing, but so quietly that all Michelle could hear was the low murmur of a man's voice.

Suddenly, something small fell out of the sky onto the windshield and shattered. An egg. A small blue egg, which had cracked—damply. Little fragments of it had shattered on the windshield, and the insides of the egg were spilling down the glass. At the center of it Michelle saw the tiny featherless body of a bird, no larger than the tip of her pinkie, and the same color. "Oh, dear," Michelle's mother said.

Michelle looked more closely, and she could see that the featherless thing, exposed on their windshield, was alive, and that it was trying to move its useless, fleshy wings. Its miniature beak was opening and closing, and Michelle's mother made a sound of horror and disgust in the back of her throat, as if she might vomit. Then she told Michelle to close her eyes and turned on the windshield wipers.

When she opened them again, they had already parked alongside Half Moon Lake.

They never talked about it—which was the strangest thing of all, because Michelle's mother loved to talk. Michelle's mother talked about everything. But this little horror—the bad dream of it, that little pulse-beat of a bird dropping out of the sky, being *born* into it too fast, too tiny, and without feathers—not another word was ever said about it.

* * *

When they step out of the plane to descend the stairs to the tarmac, the air is so full of the scent of vegetation and sea that it hardly seems to Michelle to be *air* as it turns to a film of perfumed humidity on her face and neck.

It's like a kiss, that air.

Before she starts down the stairs behind Terri and Anne, Michelle stands at the top for a few seconds and lets it kiss her, that air, until she feels she's ready to breathe it in.

eight

Anne

THE RIDE FROM the airport to the hotel was quick and wild—a buoyant careening along a road so smooth and black it seemed to have been freshly paved only days before, in a vehicle that seemed to have no shock absorbers at all, and tires so soft they rode the tar like a boat on water. There was no yellow line down the center of the road, and no other cars on it except for one wobbly bus slowly driving along the side, around which our driver swerved, honking, yelling out the window.

Through the cab windows we could see the jungle blur by—vast and dense, with lime green leaves on low-hanging branches and vines. The occasional burst of red or pink bloomed close to the ground.

Jungle, but with desert at the edges of it.

There was dry red dirt at the side of the road, and, here and there, a cactus, looking deformed and in pain, standing sentinel at the entrance to the jungle.

Although it was still early morning, it was so hot that the air seemed to pummel us as we sped through it.

No seat belts.

Had any one of the three of us ever driven anywhere, or been driven anywhere, without a seat belt on? We'd been born long after the public service announcements for that had even been needed. So, it felt like skinny-dipping, being in the back of that speeding car without a seat belt. It felt like dancing on a rooftop, or lying down on train tracks. Without seat belts, there was a loose ecstatic chaos, which could have been freedom, or danger, or both. What it meant, more than anything else, was that our mothers were nowhere around. That the adults in charge here were nothing like our parents. That we were the adults in charge now.

The jungle began to thin at the side of the road, and through the trees and vines we could see what appeared to be the ocean, except that the water was so blue it looked as if it were lit from within—more like sky than water. Not blue. *Turquoise.* Not even turquoise—but a word that had not yet been invented, in English at least, for a color none of us had ever seen.

The lobby of the Hotel del Sol wasn't air-conditioned—or, if it was, the air-conditioning was broken. There were fans whirring in each corner, and it smelled like the reptile house at the zoo—water, flesh, salt. Sprawled on the wicker couches, and sitting or lying on every inch of the tiled floor, were teenagers and college students—chatting, sleeping, fanning themselves with fashion magazines, heads resting on duffel bags, feet propped up on suitcases. Some were wearing shorts and T-shirts, or sun-dresses, but most were in bathing suits. Flowered trunks. Bikinis. And all that flesh, exposed, seemed more than naked. Lacking more than *clothes*. I hadn't seen flesh like this for months. It was March. Winter had started in Illinois in November and even before that we'd all been in pants and jackets for as long as I could remember. All this flesh looked, to me, de-furred, de-feathered, delicious.

Leaning against a pillar were two nearly naked kids. The boy's cutoffs hung so low on his hips I could see where his pubic hair began, and the girl was in a black bikini that was really no more than three small triangles held together with string. They were kissing loudly. I could hear it clearly over the whir of the fans. It was impossible to look at them, or to look away.

"Reservation numbers?" a bored-looking older woman behind the check-in desk asked.

"Oh," Terri said.

She was the one with our confirmation number because her mother was the one who'd done all the work for the trip over the internet. She opened up her purse and began to fish through it.

I sighed. Terri was always losing things in that purse.

Terri and I had become friends in fifth grade when she sat next to me, copying my homework, borrowing my pencils, breaking the points off of them, or losing them. I was the one who'd introduced her to Michelle. The two of them never became close, but they were always happy enough to hang out, and Terri became the third girl we'd call up and take along when Michelle and I were doing something that didn't exclude a third person—football games, shopping, spring break.

Terri looked up, annoyed at me for being annoyed at her, and said, "I've *got* it. Don't *worry*."

But she was still tearing through her purse, seeming unable to find it, when Michelle screamed—sharp and fast and loud—and Terri dropped her purse at her feet. Lipgloss, tampons, and scraps of paper spilled onto the floor, but we both turned around fast to see what Michelle was pointing at:

A small green flash. Something sequined and gleaming slipping over her suitcase, and then disappearing into the shadowy crack between the floor and the check-in desk.

Michelle took a step toward it, but I grabbed her arm, and the thing made a hissing sound.

"Jeez, Michelle," I said. "Were you going to touch it?"

"No," she said. "I just wanted to see it."

Our room was on the eighth floor. The balcony didn't have a view of the pool or the ocean, but even looking over the parking lot was breathtaking. Far into the distance, for miles and miles, there were pink and white hotels, cabs zipping between them, and students on spring break, crowds of them, walking along the sidewalks and in the streets. Shorts and tank tops and bikinis, bare flesh everywhere.

"*Vamos a la playa!*" Terri said.

"What does that mean?" I asked.

Terri was the only one of the three of us who knew any Spanish. Michelle and I had taken French, and hadn't even learned much of that. Our teacher, Mr. Otto, preferred to help us make posters for Pep Club rallies than to teach.

"It means let's go to the beach, stupid!"

But, by the time Michelle and I were ready to go—wearing our bathing suits, towels draped over our shoulders—Terri was lying on her side on one of the two double beds. Her mouth was open, her eyes were closed, and she was breathing steadily—deeply asleep.

nine
Michelle

THE HOTEL DEL SOL looks exactly like the matchbook-size photograph on the brochure, but so enormous that it's impossible to really see it, close up, all at once. Michelle has to squint, hold a hand over her eyes like a visor, and consider it in pieces—the balconies, the windows, the parking lot. The sliding glass doors to the lobby. The banner over those doors:

WELCOME SPRING BREAK

It is a hulking pink edifice—like some kind of little girl's toy that's mutated at the edge of the ocean, at the end of the jungle. Like something out of a fairy tale that's bloated in the sun and become both beautiful and monstrous. Even the shadow it casts is pink.

It's only 7 A.M., but already it's hot and bright. The sun is a fiery presence at the edge of the sky. There are screams and splashes coming from the other side of the hotel:

The pool.

There'd been a photograph of that, too, on the brochure—a diamond-shaped shimmering surrounded by lounge chairs. A bar with a thatched roof. A slide that looked like a smooth white tongue dipping into the water.

In the brochure, a banner had been draped between palm trees: COCKTAILS & DREAMS WELCOME PARTY 4:00.

Then, Michelle sees the ocean.

It's only a hundred feet away from where she stands when their driver from the airport drops them off in the hotel parking lot.

An expanse so blue it appears to be *painted* blue.

A blue you couldn't even really call topaz, or opal, or aquamarine.

Luminous, pure, and endless, with a hint of green in it, too—a very pale green radiating, loosely, just beneath the surface.

This hint of green makes the blue even bluer.

It is, Michelle thinks, as if this is the original

source, the place where the whole idea of *blue* began.

As the taxi driver tosses their suitcases out of the trunk and onto the sidewalk, the three girls stand together and look in the direction of that ocean, blinking.

"Oh, my god," Anne says, and touches her forehead, right between her eyes.

"It doesn't look real," Michelle says.

"Oh," Terri says, "it's so . . . *blue*."

"Duh," Anne says, and they all laugh.

It's so . . . blue.

The blue water of paradise.

Both real *and* blue.

Over the water, Michelle sees a few clouds traveling through the sky so swiftly they seem to be on film, fast-forwarded. Like clouds being chased by wind, not pushed by it.

And they're thin. Like tattered bits of silk. Or spiderweb. Or old ladies' hair.

She has no sooner seen those clouds than they're gone, swept over her head to the other side of the earth.

All her life, Michelle thinks, she's been seeing clouds, and never anything like this. The brevity of them. The incredible speed.

They're on a peninsula, she realizes, a piece of land jutting into an ocean. A spot at the edge of the world—at the ends of the earth.

Or, the place where the world ends and where it begins.

After they check in and go to their room, they stand on the balcony, and here Michelle can see even more clearly that this isn't just a playground for spring break.

Her mother was right. All of this—the sky, the ocean, the jungle—was here long before the whole idea of spring break.

And it had been sacred.

It's *still* sacred.

Beyond the miles of white and pink hotels—flashy, modern—there's that green darkness of the jungle, shivering and deep, and the sound of that water rhythmically washing against the shore. Seeing and hearing those makes the Hotel del Sol, and all the other hotels, and the students swarming between them, and even she and Anne and Terri, seem temporary to Michelle. Like afterthoughts. Like interlopers.

And the sun!

It hasn't even yet risen thoroughly in the sky, but it's already a burning crown. A dazzling god.

These are the ancient things and *they* are nothing but brief interruptions in them:

The hotels in their towering flimsiness. The American teenagers screaming in the pool, sprawled on the floor of the lounge, leaning over the balcony, taking it in.

Spring break. This week. It isn't even a blip in the scheme of things here. A fraction of a single heartbeat.

Even the view of the parking lot from the balcony makes this perfectly clear to Michelle.

ten

Anne

WE SWAM ALL morning in the ocean outside the Hotel del Sol, and well into the afternoon. Michelle and I were on our own until Terri woke up, back in the hotel room, read Michelle's note, and joined us in the water, bringing with her two snorkel masks she'd rented on the beach.

The three of us took turns wearing them—floating just under the surface of the water and breathing at the same time.

It was like a weird dream under there.

A million different kinds of fish, all lit up, fluorescent.

Like flowers that had been left in the water and grown fins and eyes.

We were amazed. We couldn't tear ourselves away.

In the turquoise light that rippled along the soft sea floor, there were fish with purple wings. Fish with babies' faces. Fish with orange, unblinking eyes. Fish that seemed to be wearing lace gowns. Fish that pulsed greenly. Shimmered with gold. Zipped past so fast it was hard to believe you'd seen anything at all—just an impression left behind of something startlingly sequined, red.

And there were clawed things crawling around in the soft sand. Rocks with legs. A school of what might have been a thousand silver fish so tiny they looked like a blizzard of petals.

There was one long, pale blue ribbon with eyes and a mouth.

There was something long and gray, which, at the same moment you saw it, burrowed into a ridge in the sand and disappeared.

Back on shore, we could hear music playing loudly (a live band?) near the pool, and spring-breakers screaming. When we looked, we could see kids on the balconies of the Hotel del Sol, high-fiving each other, tossing paper cups into the breeze. There were thousands of bodies on the beach by then—lying on towels, lying on lounge chairs, strolling, jogging, playing volleyball, holding beer bottles. Games were being played in crowds, but up there on the beach, it looked like a dull imitation of beauty, of fun—those bodies in their bright bathing suits. A pale imitation of what was going on under the ocean—that whole world below the surface—which we'd never even dreamed of, and now we could see.

None of us said anything about leaving, about going off in search of the things we'd come here to find—drinks, boys, tans—until we were so sunburned and hungry we had to leave.

Or, at least, until Michelle and I were sunburned.

Terri was the only one of us who'd had the forethought to put on sunblock before leaving the hotel. By the time Michelle and I remembered, the damage had already been done. Michelle's shoulders looked as if they'd been stung by wasps—small raised blotches scattered over her skin. And I could feel the burn all over myself, like the prickling of red ants. I could even smell it—the cooked flesh of my arms.

"Yow," Terri said, looking at me and Michelle. "That's gotta hurt. Why didn't you guys put on sunblock?"

"Oh, shut up, Terri," I said, but Michelle just nodded.

Terri was, of course, right.

How many tubes and bottles of it did we have in our suitcases between us?

Five? Seven?

How many times had each of our mothers said, "You girls remember to wear sunblock. Don't forget to put on sunblock. The sun down there isn't like the sun up here. Don't forget your *sunblock*!"

And Michelle and I had forgotten, while Terri—the acknowledged forgetful one of the three of us—hadn't.

By the time we crawled out of the ocean, the sun had already risen to the top of the sky and begun to inch its way back down. We started back toward the hotel, still blinking salt water, zigzagging through the bodies on the beach back to our flip-flops and towels, which were right where we'd left them. Terri stopped to talk to a boy with a Frisbee (he was blond, chiseled, and wearing a T-shirt that said USC on it—the college she'd be attending in the fall). When Michelle and I hesitated, waiting for her, she turned to give us a *get-lost* look.

So Michelle and I headed back to our room for showers.

When I licked my lips, I could taste the sea.

It had dried and crusted on the back of my hands, and they sparkled in the sun.

eleven

Michelle

THE COOL WATER of the shower feels terrible and wonderful on her burned back. The salt, sliding off her skin, seems to leave a fresh new layer of skin under it. When she closes her eyes, she can see it again:

Just under the surface. Psychedelic. Beautiful and scary in its strangeness. The fish, choreographed. In their elegant apparel. Swimming, wide-eyed, in slow motion, like the embodiment of dreams themselves. She'd had no idea!

It had not been like any swimming she'd ever done before, or any experience of fish she'd ever even *imagined*. Fish in the aquarium at the dentist's office. Fish swimming in circles. Or the minnows in the shallows of the freshwater lakes near home. Or even in the dark waters of the Pacific Ocean, where she'd gone swimming with her mother. That ocean had held secrets, Michelle had felt certain, but it was too cold, too black, to reveal them.

But this!

It had been as if some layer of the universe had been peeled away to reveal what was really there, just to please her. She had waited all her life to glimpse that, and—although she knows her mother will kill her when she gets home in three days with layers of her own skin burned and peeled away—it was worth it, wasn't it? It was even worth her mother's anger, the physical pain, to have seen *beneath* the surface and found it to be more dazzling and beautiful than anything she'd ever seen *above* it. Michelle hates her mother's disapproval, but sometimes it can't be avoided. Sometimes it's worth it. Like the summer afternoon when she was eight or nine years old and trying to save up her money for a pink radio she'd seen at Wal-Mart, and got permission from her mother to open an Hawaiian Punch stand in the driveway, as long as she stayed at least ten feet from the road. Her mother had given her a big plastic bottle of the punch—Technicolor and incredibly sweet—and some paper cups, and she set up a card table with a sign:

PUNCH FIFTY CENTS

She'd sold out of Hawaiian Punch within forty-five minutes. Mostly, her customers were people she knew. Loren Hayley's mother, on her way home from the gym. Mr. Graves, the janitor at their elementary school.

But her last customer had been a man she'd never seen before.

He'd pulled up in a green car and gotten out.

After Michelle poured him his cup of Hawaiian Punch, the man drank it fast, and it left a little stain at the corners of his mouth.

He smiled. He had dimples. His teeth were so white they looked like chalk, or paper. He wore a pink shirt and khaki shorts, a thin black belt threaded through the loops.

"Ah," he said, handing the empty paper cup back to Michelle. "That was worth more than fifty cents."

He reached into his back pocket, took out his wallet, and handed a green bill to her.

"Thank you," Michelle said.

"Thank *you*," he said.

He'd already pulled out of the driveway and into the street when Michelle really looked at the bill and saw that it was a twenty.

She rushed inside to show it to her mother, who looked at it. A slow shadow had crossed her face. "Who was he?" she asked.

Michelle shrugged. Just a man who wanted some Hawaiian Punch. A customer.

Michelle's mother went to the front door, and looked out. But the man had been gone a long time. When she turned around, her face seemed angry and afraid, and she said, "You can't do that again, Michelle. You can't sell Hawaiian Punch in the driveway."

Why not?

Michelle's mother had leaned over to look into Michelle's face. She talked to her for a long time. Her breath smelled like green tea. She talked about trust and healthy skepticism. About the balance between anxiety and caution. Paralyzing timidity and vigilance. She told Michelle that it was a challenge, being female. That it was hard to be the mother of a female, too—always trying to judge the line between overprotection and potential danger. She talked about being brave, but also not allowing oneself to be a victim. The difference between being fearful and being careful. That you can't go through this world fearing every man in it, but that there are bad men out there.

But the twenty-dollar bill bought both the pink radio and a sweater-skirt set for her Barbie! And those things had seemed well worth the risk to Michelle. Worth even the lecture. The way this sunburn seemed to be the price for what she'd glimpsed under the ocean while she was burning.

Still, Michelle thinks as the shower steams around her, she won't slip up again in Mexico. She knows her mother was right. She should have remembered the sunblock.

How could she have forgotten?

And what else about spring break did her mother warn her about?

Don't drink. Of course. Or, if you do, stay sober enough to take care of yourself. Look out for your friends if they get drunk.

Don't take rides, or even go on walks, with strangers.

Don't fall asleep in a public place. Don't let anyone bring you a drink from the bar that you didn't see the bartender pour himself (date rape drugs), and don't leave your wallet (identity theft) or money in the hotel room when you go out.

Don't open the hotel room door for anyone you don't know. And, remember, there will be people in Cancún from all over the country, all over the world. These people could tell you anything about themselves, and you would have no way of knowing whether or not it was true.

Out of the shower, Michelle pats her burned back gingerly with the towel and promises to herself that she'll be more careful.

For her own sake, and for her mother's.

She looks at her sunburned self in the mirror until the steam rises up, softens her image, swallows it.

twelve

Anne

IT DIDN'T TAKE us long to find Terri down at the tiki bar by the pool, although we had to push a path through the throngs.

There were kids everywhere. Sprawled on the floor in the hallway, standing in crowds near the elevators. There were couples lying together on towels. Boys wrestling over footballs, volleyballs. Girls getting piggyback rides from boys, laughing, singing, screaming. The smell of beer and perspiration on the breeze off the ocean. A hundred glistening, featureless bodies. To get lost in that crowd would be to *become* the crowd. But we managed to wind our way through it to the tiki bar.

Terri was there, still in her pink bikini, twirling on a

barstool, talking to the guy in the USC shirt. His orange swimming trunks had slipped down in back, exposing a blinding white crack of skin between his waist and his butt. There was a tattoo of a dragon on his right shoulder blade. It looked cartoonish, like a dragon from a PBS kids show, and Michelle said, "Do you think he's ever seen that tattoo?"

"Maybe he got it when he was a toddler," I said.

But Terri was leaning into him, and, even from a distance, it was clear she was drunk already. The large movements of her arms as she spoke. The way she was leaning—no, *sprawled*—across the bar, looking at her new friend. As we got closer, it became even more obvious. Her lips looked as shiny as mirrors—looser, pinker, more pouty than they were when she was sober. Terri turned then, saw us, and held up her glass. "It's called Sky Juice!" she shouted too loudly.

And it *was* the blue of the sky over Cancún—a pale, metallic blue, as if the beauty of the sky had been melted down, funneled into Terri's glass.

"Here's to the sky!" the guy beside her said, raising his Corona to her Sky Juice. He didn't even glance up at us. He was looking at Terri. He was awed by her. Rendered slack-jawed. And she did look beautiful—her blond hair tousled by the sea breeze, glistening in the sun. Her pretty, upturned nose a little pink. Her smooth muscles exposed by the bikini. She turned her back to us then, too, and it was clear she had nothing more to say. We were free to go. She was requesting, in her drunken way, that we leave her alone with her new friend. Terri collected intense, brief boyfriends. Boys she flirted with for a week and then forgot about. Or met at the pool in the summer. Or this one—who would be, I knew, the Spring Break Boy.

"Now what?" I said to Michelle.

Michelle shrugged.

We'd gotten dressed up.

Michelle was wearing a green and white sundress that her mother had bought for her to wear to her cousin's wedding the summer before. It fit better this year than it had last summer. She'd started running and doing sit-ups in September, after catching an unflattering glimpse of herself in the bathroom mirror. I'd worn my khaki skirt and a lacy pink tank top.

It was late afternoon, and the hotel had begun making announcements over a loudspeaker that "Hedonistic Happy Hour" would start in the Hotel del Sol lounge at four o'clock. The announcements were fuzzy but deafeningly loud, delivered in English with a heavy Spanish accent. After each announcement, a roar of shouting and applause followed.

There would also be "Pirate Poison Shots" by the pool. *Yeah!!!*

Body shots at the tiki bar. *Whhooooooo!*

Wet T-shirt contest on the beach. *Awwraaaaaaa!!!!*

Three-legged tequila race. *Owowowow!!*

Already, the sun had begun to dip in the sky. No one was lying on the beach any longer, soaking up the sun, although most were still in their bathing suits. The hotel grounds, and the inside of the hotel, were swarming with girls in bikini tops and cutoffs, swearing at one another, slamming into each other, screaming with laughter as they stumbled, spilling their drinks. There were boys, smelling of coconut oil, pumping their fists in the air, tossing sandals and towels at each other. A general rumble of music and shouting. The smell of beer and perspiration.

"Maybe we should go to the lounge?" Michelle said.

What else was there to do?

"Okay," I said. "Let's go to the lounge."

thirteen
Michelle

THE LOUNGE OF the Hotel del Sol pounds with music. A woman's voice, singing in Spanish, is drowned out by electronic instruments. And it's hot. All the little tables are crowded with girls in tube tops and tank tops and guys who are either shirtless or in T-shirts, leaning into one another's sunburned faces, shouting over the music. Anne points to the only empty table, right under the black box of a stereo speaker. "Over there!" she shouts, and Michelle follows her to it.

The floors are shiny and, although it isn't yet dark, the sun has begun to sink over the horizon. It streams through a wall of windows, bathing the lounge in blue-gray light. It isn't pleasant, somehow.

It's as if the beauty of the sky over Cancún has been filtered through something ugly, and this blue-gray light is the result. The music is deafening. It drums against her stomach, her ribs. It makes her squint, although she doesn't know why.

"Are we going to have a drink?" Michelle shouts over their tiny table to Anne after they sit down.

Anne shrugs. "I guess," she shouts. "Sky Juice?"

"Sky Juice!" Michelle shouts back.

"You're my adventurer," Michelle's mother said to her while she was packing up her bag for spring break.

But, really, Michelle wondered, what adventures had she ever had? Sure, she'd climbed some rocks with her mother in Oregon, but it wasn't like scaling sheer cliffs—just the tennis shoes and water-bottle variety of rock climbing.

And, with the exception of that, and now this, what else?

What *could* she have done?

It wasn't even safe, she'd been told over and over, to walk down your own street after dusk if you were a girl. Waiting on the corner for the city bus at twilight was a risk. Talking to a stranger in the park.

Accepting a Pepsi from a guy if you hadn't seen him pour it from the bottle.

On the other hand, there were boys from Glendale High who'd done things like hitchhike to Toronto. Who'd spent the night in a cave in Colorado. Who'd gone camping in Wyoming, or gotten into fights in bars up north.

But what adventures were there for girls to have? None of the girls Michelle knew had been on any adventures beyond spring break in Bermuda, Cancún. Or heartbreaks and flings with their friends' boyfriends. Or passing out at parties. Or skinny-dipping in the local lakes. It wasn't possible for a girl to tramp off into the forest alone, or sail across an ocean, or even pitch a tent in her own backyard after dark. Girls' adventures took place at the mall. You gave some older boy from another school district your phone number. Or shoplifted a lipstick at The Body Shop. *This* adventure—Cancún, spring break—was the closest Michelle had ever come to something real, and now she was in a lounge not that different from her basement at home.

"No," she says to Anne suddenly, who doesn't question it. "Let's just go."

They stand up at the same time.

Michelle nods at the door, and they get up and hurry out of the lounge.

"Jesus," Anne says when they're finally out and the lounge doors swing closed behind them. The sudden cessation of noise is deafening. "Let's stay out of there."

Now, the area around the pool is nearly deserted—only one couple, in the hot tub, so consumed with their kissing that they look like a single body in the bubbling water.

On the other side of a stand of palm trees, beyond the tiki bar, some game is apparently taking place, and it seems that everyone who'd been swimming in the pool or lounging beside it has gathered in a huge circle on the beach.

With the sun lower in the sky, the air seems a bit lighter and less damp—although the smell of ocean and jungle still hovers over it all, perfumed and exotic, but also a little stifling, as if the ocean has diffused and filled the air.

There's a wide banner strung up between the pool and a palm tree on the beach. BE SAFE! TROJANS! with a purple profile of a warrior in a helmet, looking blankly in the direction of the ocean.

"Should we go see what that's all about?" Anne asks, nodding toward the beach.

"No," Michelle says. "Let's skip that."

fourteen

Anne

AT THE TIKI bar, there was no one left but a man in a white shirt and khaki pants (blond, older, also sunburned), and he and the bartender (a Mexican boy in a sleeveless yellow shirt with a sunburst on it and, in red letters beneath the sunburst, HOTEL DEL SOL in red script) were sharing a joke. The bartender was laughing so hard he had to hold a hand to his eyes—to keep himself from crying? The blond man leaned backward, guffawing loudly but pleasantly. On the bar in front of him was a Sky Juice.

"There's our Sky Juice," Michelle said, walking toward the tiki bar.

I followed.

The drink was sweet. Without ice, it tasted, at room temperature, the way the ocean might have tasted without salt, I thought. Extremely blue. The blond man in the white shirt looked over at us and said, "Don't drink too many, girls."

He held up a finger and wagged it in our direction.

He was handsome, but much older. In his forties. Maybe even in his fifties. He had a foreign accent, but it wasn't Spanish. (Polish? Russian?) He spoke to us in English, then turned back to the bartender and spoke to him quickly and easily in Spanish.

I drank half of the Sky Juice too quickly—I was so thirsty—and then I pushed it away, to pace myself. I felt lightheaded already, but that could as easily have been from the sun, the swimming, and not having slept for twenty-four hours, as from Sky Juice, which didn't taste like wine, or beer, or whiskey—all of which I'd had and none of which I particularly liked. This was perfect. Just sweet enough, and no burning on the back of my throat after I swallowed.

There were screams and squeals coming from the crowd of kids on the beach. By now there were maybe a hundred, two hundred, kids out there, pushing closer to one another, narrowing their circle around something at the center. It was impossible to tell what was happening. Just the backs of the audience. Skin. Bare male torsos, bikini straps, limbs—and, beyond that, the sea growing grayer as the sun set farther behind us.

"You are on spring break?" the blond man asked without looking at us. He was sitting across from us, but he was also looking in the direction of the crowd on the beach. He was thin, and his teeth were very white. He was deeply tanned, and his hair was so blond he looked as if he'd been outside in the sun for many years. Around his eyes there were threadlike white lines. It seemed he'd been squinting, too, for years, in the sun. Even his lips were tan. The sleeves of his white shirt were rolled up, and the hair on his arms was also bleached to a very pale blond.

"Yep," I said. "We're seniors."

"At university?" he asked, and we both laughed and looked at each other, then said no, no, we were in high school.

"Oh," he said. "Little girls." He looked at the bartender, who shrugged. *"Niñas,"* the man said to the bartender, and then something else in Spanish. And then he turned back to us. "How did you find yourself on such a trip?"

We shrugged, both of us smiling shyly, still flattered that he'd thought we were so much older than we were. Michelle took another sip of her Sky Juice, and I wondered, now, if the bartender might take our drinks away, ask for identification. But he wasn't even looking at us. He'd moved to the other side of the bar and was wiping down the counter with a very bright white cloth. When we didn't answer, the man said, "I have two daughters older than you."

"Really?" Michelle asked. She looked up from her Sky Juice at him quickly when he said this. Her eyes, looking at his, were equal in their blueness, and I realized for the first time (drunkenly, perhaps) that Michelle's eyes were sometimes the color of a robin's egg and sometimes a pale stone-green. The stranger's were, at the moment, robin's egg blue, too.

"Twenty and twenty-two," the stranger said. He smiled a little wistfully into his own Sky Juice then, as if just saying their ages had brought them fondly to mind. "And you girls—where are your fathers, that they send you off on a trip to Mexico for your spring break? They have not heard what can happen to girls in such places?"

fifteen
Michelle

WITHOUT HAVING BEEN asked, the bartender brings Michelle another Sky Juice and places it in front of her, removing the straw from her old one and putting it in the new before taking her empty glass away.

From the crowd on the beach there's a burst of wild laughter and screaming again. The screaming startles a flock of seagulls and they rise up flying, also screaming, away down the shore, pumping their white wings hard against the sea breeze. The water looks full of blue feathers, shining and churning under the sun—as if layers of feathers are tucked there between the sky and whatever it is below that blue.

It's easy enough to imagine *anything* under the surface of that.

Serpents. Castles. Cathedrals. Whole civilizations.

It's hard to imagine that it could ever be dark under there, to believe that, although the sun doesn't reach the depths, there isn't some other, some *better,* source of light beneath that brilliant surface.

Michelle hasn't really looked at the stranger across from them at the bar until he mentions that he has two daughters, because she hasn't wanted him to think she was flirting with him. She's made that mistake before. At the State Fair the summer before, she asked a man who was taking tickets at the Ferris wheel if people ever got so scared on the ride that it had to be stopped. She'd been feeling lighthearted, having just stepped off the Tilt-A-Whirl, and she was waiting for Anne and Terri to finish eating their snow cones so they could go on the ride together. She'd also just been curious, and wanted to make conversation with the man as they stood together in the dark watching the slowly turning wheel, its lights and buckets swaying in the deep indigo of an August night.

But the ticket taker had turned all the way around to look at her, to take in her breasts and legs. She'd been wearing skimpy summer clothes—cutoffs, a tank top with a sailboat on it, sandals. "Yeah," he said. "Sometimes. Why?"

"Just curious," Michelle had said, and started to walk away, to go back to Terri and Anne and their snow cones near the concession stand, but he called after her, "Hey, baby, don't go. We were just getting to know each other."

Michelle started to walk faster then. She could still hear him calling loudly to her, but not what he was saying. Her heart was pounding in her throat. "We can't go on the Ferris wheel," she told Anne and Terri. After she told them why, they agreed to go on the Blizzard with her instead—a screaming propulsion, throbbing to disco music. But when they'd stumbled off of it, the Ferris wheel ticket taker was waiting for them—for *her*.

"Hi again, sweetheart," he'd said to Michelle.

He was smoking a cigarette. He looked old, and mean. Sneering, blowing smoke out his nose. His teeth were brown, and there were deep lines etched down the center of his face. He was like something hideous out of a fairy tale. When Michelle tried to hurry past him, he grabbed her arm hard, and she twisted away, saying, *"Don't,"* in a voice that surprised her with its meekness. She wasn't even sure she'd said it loudly enough for him to hear.

But he had. *"Don't,"* he said, in a mocking, mousy voice.

Right after that, the three girls left the fair together, rushing out of the gate despite the fifteen dollars they'd each paid for the paper bracelets that would let them go on as many rides as they wanted.

Since then, Michelle had been more careful.

She didn't make eye contact with the guy behind the counter at the video store because she could tell how much he wanted her to. She didn't let her eyes meet those of the old man who worked behind the reference desk at the library. She didn't even look into the face of Mr. Brecht, the choir director and her voice teacher, because one day when she was singing "Ave Maria" she looked over to find him gazing up at her from the piano bench with such joy and admiration it had scared her. It was just the music, she supposed, but she had no way of knowing for sure, and she didn't want to take a chance.

Her beauty, she knew, was nothing like Terri's—that bleached blonde, with the big breasts and big smile that caused males and females equally, and of all ages, to stare at her when she crossed a room. And she had none of Anne's freckled cuteness. But men seemed attracted to Michelle. They seemed to think she was older than she was, and would ask her where she went to college or where she worked—as if she might already be done with college. She'd never wanted such attention. It had always come as a terrible surprise.

So, it's a relief that the stranger at the tiki bar tells them he has two daughters older than she and Anne. A man with two daughters in their teens or twenties would not misunderstand the intentions of girls that age, would he? And now, too, he's been told that they are only in high school, so he can't mistake them for older girls. He knows they aren't flirting with him, that their friendliness is only that—friendliness.

Michelle looks up from her Sky Juice, looks across at the stranger, smiling, answering his questions—and when she does, when she really looks at him for the first time, she's shocked to see how blue his eyes are.

For a moment, it surprises her into silence. Seeing his eyes, she takes a startled little breath. His eyes have caught her off guard. Has she ever in her life, she wonders, seen such blue eyes?

sixteen

Anne

MY FATHER ALWAYS said of Michelle, "That little girl wants a daddy."

Until I got older, I never understood what he meant, because Michelle was so shy around men. When my own dad would come home from work, if Michelle and I were in the living room playing with Barbies or at the kitchen table giggling and eating cookies, she'd go completely silent. She'd stop whatever she was doing and put her hands in her lap. When my father said, "Hello, girls," she'd mumble politely, but mostly she seemed just to want to get away.

Later, it was the same with our gym teacher, Mr. Wiknowski. And even Mr. Otto, in French class.

And her choir director, Mr. Brecht. The same girl who would have been laughing hysterically in the locker room, wearing her gym shorts on her head, would go completely quiet in the gym when Mr. Wiknowski said hello.

But by then I'd figured it out. How shy, and how full of longing, an older man made her. Once, I'd caught her looking at a photograph of me and my dad in the pool in our backyard. I was eleven or twelve in that photo, and he'd hoisted me out of the water and was getting ready to toss me backward into it again, and we were both laughing. Michelle was hovering over it at my dresser, squinting into it, and I knew then that she was trying to imagine herself in that picture, and couldn't. Once, I asked her if she was sad about not having a father, or not knowing who her father was. She just said, "I'm always looking," and I knew she meant that the looking was the bad part. Not the *not having*, but the blank space always waiting to be filled.

"So, you girls, how long are you to stay in Mexico?"

We told him we were on a four-day/three-night charter. And today was the first day.

He laughed. He said, "So, you plan to see only this?" He gestured to the beach, the crowd of whooping students on it. They'd begun to disperse, wandering away from whatever had been at the center of the crowd. "And," he said, "to drink Sky Juice?"

The bartender brought me a second drink soon after bringing Michelle's, and I felt suddenly ashamed to have it. The first one had already made me tipsy. Now that the crowd on the beach had broken up, some of the kids who'd been in it were stumbling back toward the bar, and I could see how drunk they were. One girl was being held up between two friends, dragging her legs in the sand, stumbling, laughing loudly. Her bikini top had slipped down over one of her breasts, and she wasn't bothering to do anything about it. I pushed the drink a few inches away from me.

"No," Michelle said. "We want to see the Mayan ruins, too. The pyramid. At Chichén Itzá."

"Chee-chun Eet-sa." He corrected her pronunciation. "In that case, you are in luck. I am here, myself, for that purpose only, and if you would like a ride and a guide, I am going to the site tomorrow.

I am a historian, by profession. An archaeologist, as a hobbyist."

Michelle and I exchanged glances.

Could we?

My sunburn had begun to prickle hotly across my shoulders, as if in answer to the question hanging in the air between us. As if my mother were tapping me on the back, on my sunburn, reminding me of the things I'd promised not to do on spring break. Sunburn. Strangers. Rides.

"But," the stranger said, "if I were your fathers I would say do not take a ride to the ruins with a stranger! And if my own daughters were to do so, I would be furious. And still, I offer you tomorrow morning, if you are ready by sunrise, a ride to the ruins in my rental car. Maybe then I make up for being a stranger giving you a ride by saving you from drinking any more Sky Juice tonight. Because then you must go to bed now. Sunrise here is five o'clock in the morning."

I looked over at Michelle. She was looking carefully into the face of the stranger, as if trying to read his thoughts. Then she looked down, into her Sky Juice, and shook her head just a little so that only I could have seen it. She'd made our decision for us. No.

It was a relief in a way, but I was also a little disappointed. A free ride in a car instead of on a bus—and we were going anyway. And this man no longer seemed like a stranger to me. Or at least not the kind of stranger who would rape us, leave our bodies in the jungle. Except for his accent, this stranger reminded me of our history teacher, Mr. Bardot, who was also an amateur archaeologist. In September he'd forced our class to sit through four weeks of slides from his various expeditions. Greece. Turkey. Guatemala. The Upper Peninsula. A bog in Scotland.

He never found, it seemed to us, anything of interest on any of these trips. A shard of bone in the bog, where he'd been looking for sacrificial victims, which turned out just to be the back of a pigeon's skull. A link from a bracelet near an ancient tomb in Greece. (That one turned out to be from the fifties.) Mr. Bardot laughed about it, but remained, it seemed, so passionate about his hobby and all the treasures he'd never found that, despite myself, I'd also become intrigued by the washed-out slides of dirt and rocks in foreign places.

Neither this stranger at the tiki bar nor Mr. Bardot was, I felt sure, the kind of stranger our mothers would have worried about. But I couldn't go without Michelle, so I didn't have to feel sorry about it anyway, I thought. The crowd from the beach had begun to swarm the tiki bar. They were shouting at the bartender, pushing against us, between us, smelling of sweat and coconut oil and alcohol. And then Michelle looked up, pushing the half-finished second Sky Juice away from herself, stood, and said, "Okay, maybe."

The stranger looked surprised. He raised his eyebrows. He said, "Well, then, I am leaving for my dinner appointment now, so I will just tell you that if you are at the front desk at 5:20 A.M., no later, I will take you tomorrow and bring you back before bedtime. And if you drink and sleep too late, and I do not see you again, I wish that you have a safe and grand vacation, and that you girls behave yourselves."

He pushed his chair away from the bar then, and a beefy-looking boy in a Nirvana T-shirt slid into his chair. The stranger left some Mexican money near his glass. He said, *"Adiós, amigo,"* to the bartender, who was pouring a shot of tequila for a girl who looked about fourteen, and very drunk.

"Let's go," Michelle said.

Walking away from the tiki bar, I said, "No way. We're not driving off with some guy we met at the bar. It's exactly what you're not supposed to do on spring break."

Michelle said, noncommittally, "Probably not. You're probably right."

"You said '*maybe*,'" I said. "I think he took that as a yes."

"Well," Michelle said, "'*Maybe*' isn't '*yes*,' and even if it is we can change our minds. If you think it's a bad idea, let's forget it. I thought you were the one who wanted to go with him."

"Why?" I asked. "What made you think that?"

"Because you were smiling at him," Michelle said. "And the whole time he was talking you were nodding at him like you were ready to go anywhere he wanted."

Was it true?

I supposed it was.

Already, I realized, I'd forgotten the twinge of

disappointment I'd felt when I thought Michelle had shaken her head no.

But then, when she'd said *maybe*, the stupidity of it had seemed clear to me. Now it occurred to me that perhaps Michelle and I had always made our decisions like this. *The mall or the movie? To stay at the party, or leave?* We were always watching the other one, wondering, and then challenging, and then . . .

"Let's forget it," Michelle said. "If you think it's a bad idea, let's take the bus."

"Do you think it's a bad idea?"

"I think," Michelle said, "he seemed pretty safe."

"They always seem safe," I said. "That's what they all said about Ted Bundy. That he was the most normal-seeming guy in the world."

"That's true," Michelle said. "But that's what they say about most men who are normal, too."

"That's true," I said.

"But I'll do whatever you think," Michelle said.

"What do *you* think?" I asked her.

Again, she shrugged.

So, in the end, neither of us made the decision, but we both knew that we were taking a ride to Chichén Itzá with a stranger in the morning.

seventeen

Michelle

THEY HAVEN'T EATEN dinner, so they buy crackers, juice, and four granola bars in the gift shop and take them back out to the pool.

There are no kids out there anymore. They've gone, it seems, to other bars. There isn't even any music booming from the balconies of the hotel. It's as if Michelle and Anne have been left behind, abandoned in the ruins of a lost civilization.

They lie down in lounge chairs at the side of the pool. Over the chlorinated water, the moon travels like some kind of supernatural soccer ball—pale and rippling as the breeze off the ocean stirs the pool. The breeze has gotten stronger since the sun set.

The crackers and granola bars are a perfectly

sufficient dinner. Why, Michelle wonders, do people bother with all that cooking and cleaning? She thinks of all the trouble her mother goes to every night to provide a well-rounded meal, but all you really need is a handful of Ritz Bits, a container of juice, and two oatmeal raisin bars.

"You eat like a bird," her mother has always told her—but why not eat like a bird?

A peck at this, a peck at that.

These bits and sips make her feel lighter, freer, than a potato and a piece of tofu. She hasn't eaten meat since she was in third grade and suddenly realized, biting into a hamburger, that it was a *cow.*

The sound of the breeze (is it, now, wind?) is both completely, rhythmically, peaceful and violent. If it weren't so warm, the roughness of it on their exposed skin would have chafed them. Michelle can hear it rattling the fronds on the roof of the tiki bar, flapping the fabric of the Trojans banner, and the one that says WELCOME SPRING BREAK.

She is about to say something to Anne about tomorrow. About the stranger. She knows that, in a way, they've already decided, and that Anne thinks it's because of the free ride, and the ruins, and because it's no way to live, being afraid of everyone all the time.

But Michelle also knows that she wants to go because of his eyes, and that she should tell Anne.

When she was in kindergarten, Michelle had come home one afternoon after Doughnuts for Dads Day—a day in which fathers stopped by their kids' classrooms on the way to or from work, lured by the bait of pastry—and Michelle had said to her mother, "I want a daddy."

"Maybe you do, maybe you don't," her mother had said without even blinking. "There are all kinds of daddies, and they're not all good. Some of them are. But you'll never have one."

At first, Michelle had wanted to cry. The bluntness of her mother's answer. It was, perhaps, the first time Michelle had really realized that she would never have one—a father. Until then, it had seemed possible that a father might find her, or she might find him—mysteriously, suddenly, and with no real search. The way other children seemed to simply *have* fathers. As if there were nothing unusual about it at all.

But she didn't cry. She couldn't even *make* herself

cry. It was strange. It was as if her mother, saying those last words on the subject of a father, had cast a spell, had waved a wand over Michelle's heart—and in that moment she went from a fairy tale castle, locked in a tower, longing for a father, to being a scientist, a researcher, a physicist of fathers.

Now, although she still longed to find her sperm, longed to have a father, she was able to be completely objective, too, about her longing.

The next year on Doughnuts for Dads Day, Michelle was able to appraise the fathers. The grim-looking dads. The overly robust dads. The self-conscious ones, the ones who looked too young to be dads, the weary-looking ones. Mixed in were some who seemed plainly good and kind, and she liked them well enough, but she didn't bother to dwell on that, because they weren't hers and never would be.

Still, there were habits of the heart she never broke. And one of them was that when she saw a man with blue-green eyes, or a man who played the cello, or had curly dark hair, as her mother had told her about the sperm she'd chosen, Michelle couldn't help but wonder.

Of course, of those attributes, the stranger at the tiki bar had only the blue-green eyes, and, because her sperm had donated himself in Glendale, Illinois, eighteen years before, it seemed unlikely that she would find him here in Cancún, with a Polish or Russian accent. And still, she couldn't help it—that vague calling for connection between her DNA and the universe out of which it had spilled down to her, to create her.

It's why she didn't just say no to the stranger, to taking a ride to the Mayan ruins with him. It was why she wanted to go, despite everything she knew about strangers, and rides with them.

Anne says something about getting ready to go to bed because they'll need to get up early to meet their ride, and then the strongest gust yet blows over a table on the other side of the pool, and then, as if it had all just been a candle flicker, the lights of the Hotel del Sol go out—the lights from the rooms, the lights strung between the palm trees, and, when she sits up and looks around her, Michelle sees that the lights of all the hotels along the shore, the whole long line of them, are simply blown out, and they're plunged into a darkness so total that the pool fills completely and suddenly with rippling stars, just like the sky.

Anne and Michelle both gasp when it happens, but when they realize what it is, that the wind has blown the power out, they adjust to the darkness and lie back in it, letting it throb around them. Except for the first few exclamations ("What the—" "Holy shit" "The power's out"), they don't speak. They just settle back with their vending machine snacks and listen to the wind and the silence and the crashing of water on the shore.

It's possible, Michelle thinks with a thrill like flying, to really *feel*, to *understand*, how far from home they are.

It had only taken one plane ride but, she realizes now, the impression given by that quick trip through the air—that they were only seven hours from home, that the world was small, that they could turn around and go back in the blink of an eye—had been false.

They were *very far* from home.

If they had set out to get to this spot from where they'd started, by foot, or in a little boat, it would have taken them years. It might have cost them their lives. The people who'd lived here for centuries, before motors and jets, had been at the edge of a vast ocean, alone, in a strange and ancient world in which the waves had been crashing against the shore for as long as there had been anyone to hear it.

Longer.

Much longer.

The blue sky and the blue sea weren't just a backdrop to the Hotel del Sol. They did not just provide a beach for American teenagers to play volleyball on. They were enormous churning mysteries, and they'd been here first. And they would be here long after the American teenagers had gone home from spring break.

After all, these kids were just a snapshot of a crowd of tanned, drunk students on a beach. Holding beer bottles, plastic cups with pineapple and umbrellas floating on the top. Laughing. Bellybutton rings glinting in the sun. A flash of time, passed.

Long after, even, those snapshots were buried, and the hotels had washed away, and the jungle had crept back to the edge of the oceans, and the language they'd spoken to one another had been forgotten.

With the electricity out, and no one around, it is

possible to imagine having been the first girl to see it, Michelle thinks. To find yourself on the Yucatán Peninsula surrounded by a jungle of animals and birds, in the darkness, alone at the edge of all that mystery—until the lights flicker on again, then surge, and stay on, and it's all much brighter than it ever was before.

two

one

Anne

TERRI WASN'T IN our room when we got there. But it was only ten o'clock. Michelle and I had wanted to get to bed early, as the stranger had advised us. And we were both exhausted. The sun, the swimming, the Sky Juice—and neither of us had slept at all in over thirty hours.

We took the same bed, leaving the other for Terri—if and when.

It wasn't a problem. Michelle and I had been sharing a double bed during sleepovers since first grade. And we were both quiet sleepers, each of us happy to teeter at opposite edges of a bed so as not to bother the other. I never moved at all in my sleep. My mother told me that when I was little she'd put a blanket over me, tuck it in, slip a stuffed animal under my arm, and when she came in to wake me in the morning for preschool, I'd be exactly as she'd left me.

I fell asleep, and did not have a single dream—the night just slid out from under me, and then it was over. When the alarm began to beep at 4:55 A.M., Michelle reached over and slapped it off, and I opened my eyes.

It was dark in the room, but under the crack between the window and the curtain a bit of pink light was already seeping in. In it, I could see Terri in the bed next to ours. She was lying on her back, still in her pink bikini, on top of the covers, her arms tossed out at her sides as if she'd been crucified on the bed, or had just dropped out of the sky. I'd never heard her come in, but, from the looks of it, she hadn't done anything other than flop onto the bed when she did.

"Terri?" I whispered.

She rolled onto her side and groaned.

I took the blanket and bedspread off our bed and put it over her. I leaned over and said, "We're going to the—"

"Shhh," she said. "Please. Let me sleep. Just go."

I looked at Michelle, who shrugged.

We took turns taking quick showers, then put on shorts, T-shirts, tennis shoes. After we closed the door to the hotel room behind us and we were out in the hallway, Michelle said, "So, we're doing it? We're going?"

I shrugged.

In the elevator, she said, mostly to herself, "He seems really nice."

"He's got two daughters," I said.

"Still," Michelle said, looking at me seriously, "he's a total stranger. And we're in a foreign country."

"You're right," I said. "We shouldn't."

"But you want to, don't you?"

"Well, I guess, yeah. I thought you wanted to."

Before we had time to say any more, the doors to the elevator shuddered open, and we saw him there, standing at the desk to the Hotel del Sol, wearing a khaki cap, holding a map, and speaking in Spanish to one of the women at the front desk who'd checked us in the morning before. When he saw us, he waved.

two

Michelle

THE STRANGER'S NAME is Ander. He says to the woman at the front desk in English, when the girls walk over, "I want you to know I am taking these girls to Chichén Itzá with me." He turns then to Anne and Michelle and says, "It is not such a good idea to take a ride from a stranger, girls. But now there is a witness that I have you, so you can be a bit more assured."

Anne and Michelle both smile, laugh a little, out of embarrassment. Had he overheard them talking? Had he seen them exchange glances at the tiki bar?

But he doesn't smile. He isn't joking. The woman behind the desk says, "Okay." She is the same woman who was there when they checked in the morning before, and she still looks weary. Had she left and returned, or has she been behind that desk since then?

Ander's car is a green Renault—a make of car Michelle hasn't seen before. It's sporty, foreign looking, and she wishes, instantly, that her mother were here to see it. Despite having had only one car Michelle's entire life, her mother has always liked unusual-looking cars.

Inside, the Renault smells like sun and dust and some kind of tropical fruit. Anne slips into the backseat, so Michelle takes the passenger seat. Before they'd left the hotel lounge, Ander had insisted that the girls go to the gift shop and buy themselves two bottles of water each. ("Dehydration is a very serious thing," he had said.)

"Now," Ander says as he starts up the car and puts his sunglasses on, "the adventure begins."

In the mirror attached to the passenger-side door, Michelle watches the Hotel del Sol grow smaller and smaller as they drive away from it. A small pink castle, like something a little girl would be given for her birthday. Along with a miniature knight. A tiny princess. A fingernail-size white horse.

"It's okay to have windows unrolled until it is too hot? Or do you girls need air-conditioning, to worry about your hair?"

"No," they both answer him at once. "That's fine." He presses a button and all four windows roll down, filling the car with wind.

"So!" he shouts over it. "You've told me your names and where you are from, but what is it you do? What is it you love?"

First, he looks for an answer from Anne in the rearview mirror. She hesitates. She likes to read, she says. She wants, maybe, to be a writer.

Ander nods seriously. He looks into the rearview mirror so intently it is as if he is assessing her for the job. Then, he seems to agree that, yes, she will be a writer, and turns to Michelle beside him. "And you?"

Michelle looks away from him, out the window. The stretch of hotels has given way quickly to jungle. Now on both sides there is the rushing green darkness. She shrugs. She says, "I like to sing. I don't know. I like to travel. I like to fly. Maybe I'll be a flight attendant, and teach music?"

She looks back to Ander.

Her heart is fluttering oddly in her chest.

Why?

Is she waiting for his approval? Afraid he won't give it to her, the way he gave it to Anne?

Something about him, she thinks, makes it seem possible that he could give or refuse permission for such future dreams.

"Oh!" he says, laughing. "Very good. And how long have you been a bird?"

It takes Michelle a minute to realize what he means—that she likes to fly, and to sing. And then she laughs, too, but he's still looking at her—more seriously now—as if really waiting for an answer.

"Well," she says, "I liked to sing even when I was . . . I don't know. A toddler?"

It's true.

She has a memory of being in the backseat of her mother's car, singing along to a song she'd heard once or twice on the radio. When it was over, her mother turned to look at Michelle with an astonished expression. She said, "Sweetheart, you have the most beautiful voice."

Did she?

Later, her mother made a recording of Michelle singing "America the Beautiful," and when she played it back, Michelle could hear, too, that it was pitch-perfect, confident, a strong, clear voice.

When she was a bit older, her mother had told her that her sperm had been a musician, and slowly, over the years, Michelle began to realize that this voice was a link, through time, to him. That she had not been the first one to have this music in her. That it had started with him. Or even further back. Back to his mother? Back to his own sperm?

And back, and back, and back—to who?

His ancestry had been French and Scottish, her mother had told her—so, back to some medieval village? A washerwoman cleaning cobblestones with a rag, singing a song?

Well, Michelle would never know, but, since her mother didn't sing and neither did her mother's parents, she knew it was a link to those strangers who didn't even know (even her sperm—because how could he?) that she existed. And it was what made her different from most people. A thing she had—like Anne's writing, or Terri's beauty—that was unique to her, that she could carry around with her. She always knew that, in a line at the grocery store, or at the food court in the mall, she could make all the people within the sound of her voice put down whatever it was they'd been reading or sipping, to close their mouths on whatever last word they'd been about to speak, and turn in her direction, amazed.

She never does it, of course.

She never takes anybody by surprise by bursting into song in a public place. She's far too shy for that. But it's good, knowing that she could.

Michelle only manages to say a few of these things out loud, but to what she has said, Ander is nodding, as if he's made a decision about her, and the answer is yes.

three

Anne

WE WERE DRIVING inland, Ander told us. Had we looked at a map? Did we know where we were?

No.

He took a folded map out of the glove compartment for us and handed it to Michelle. She studied it for a few minutes and then passed it back to me.

"You see," he said, gesturing out the window at the jungle passing by, "you are in a sacred place here. Its god is Quetzalcoatl. *Ket-sah-co-ah-tul.* He is the feathered serpent, you know."

We both nodded.

"*Quetzl* is a bird that lives here, in the mists, with beautiful green tail feathers. *Coatl* is a snake. As a god, Quetzalcoatl, he is 'the wind, the breath of life, the eyes that are unseen, like the stars by day.'"

He looked at each of us in turn then and said, "I am quoting from D. H. Lawrence here." He laughed at our expressions, and then went on. "You see, Quetzalcoatl has been here for ten thousand years, and his faces change with each new period of history. Now, he is in the sky, and in the trees, trying to protect them from what this new, terrible culture of greed and debauchery would like to do to them. Sometimes, Quetzalcoatl is a peaceful, content god. But he is not now."

Ander told us this as if it were a fact, not a story, and I felt a bit of cold sweat form at the base of my neck. As it zigzagged down my spine I told myself that, no, there was nothing wrong. Ander was an anthropologist, right? He would, of course, tell stories like this. We were students to him. He was teaching us—not crazy.

Or, had we made a mistake?

I couldn't think about that now—not here, in the backseat of his car, in the jungle, speeding farther and farther away from Cancún and Terri and the Hotel del Sol. I folded up the map on my lap and put it beside me on the car seat, put the tips of my fingers on the door handle, and looked at it.

Once, I'd heard a story about a girl who, while hitchhiking, had been picked up by a man and hadn't realized until too late that there were no handles on the doors, and that the windows could not be rolled down, and that she couldn't get out.

There *were* handles on the doors of this car, and the windows were already down, but I thought about that girl and wondered—did she realize, right away, the mistake she'd made? Or did it dawn on her gradually? When was it that she'd thought to look, to see if there were door handles? Did the driver say something that made her look, or did she realize, the moment the door was closed, that she would never be leaving that car, and how stupid she'd been, long after it would have done her any good even to scream?

Michelle was looking out the passenger-side window, and the air blowing through it whipped her hair around. Usually she was so careful about her hair, smoothing it into place whenever it was mussed even a little, or gathering it in her hand when it was windy, but now she was just letting it fly all around her in a dark tangle, her arm resting on the open window, watching the jungle pass by. I wished I could ask her what she was thinking. Was she also a little afraid?

Michelle, is this man dangerous? Should we ask him to take us back? But it was impossible to talk to her. And what would I have said, anyway, in front of Ander?

I just kept my fingers on the door handle. The bead of sweat traveled all the way to the base of my spine, and eventually evaporated.

Ander went on:

"He is god of sun and water. As a child, he was so good and light he did not need wings to fly to the sky, but climbed a ladder of spiderwebs. Then, he was banished from the earth, but he always returns. You know," Ander said, "that Montezuma believed the invading Spanish ship was Quetzalcoatl, returning? Cortés landed at the exact spot where prophecy said the feathered serpent would arrive when he came back, in the exact year he was to return—1519. So, Cortés was welcomed instead of killed. It was a terrible mistake. Cortés was not Quetzalcoatl."

Ander looked at the side of Michelle's face, and then into the backseat at me, and winked.

"You must be careful," he said. "Not all who come smiling and offering treasure mean well."

When he turned back to his driving, I touched Michelle's shoulder. I was going to whisper to her, if I could, *We have to get out of this car.* But when she turned to look at me she was smiling, and her blue eyes were so bright I knew she was exactly where she wanted to be, and that somehow scared me the most.

four

Michelle

THIS IS THE first real adventure of her life. The one she's waited eighteen years to have. The one she was born to have.

As Ander drives them farther from Cancún, and the ocean, and the hotels, the road becomes rutted, and he has to slow down, bumping over the holes. It gives Michelle a chance to really look out the window and see the jungle.

It isn't as dark in there as she'd thought it would be.

True, it's full of shadows, but there's also light—sun streaming lime green through the leaves. And movement. Birds. And their screeching. And flowers. All different colors. Some on large stalks, some crawling on vines up the trunks of trees. Reds and pinks. Yellow, pale blue. Their scent travels into the car windows, dense and fleshy, along with the smell of leaves, water condensed and lingering in treetops—green things saturated and swollen.

Ander has a wonderful accent and voice. The voice is deep, and Michelle likes the sound of his vowels rolling at the top of his mouth before they leave it. And his story of the Plumed Serpent. Her mother had told her about it, too—the temple to Quetzalcoatl at Chichén Itzá, where the sacrifices to him had been made. She'd shown Michelle a painting of a creature with a turquoise beak and a snake's body—a kind of dragon, but with the arms and legs of a man.

It was gaudy, Michelle had thought then. But now, seeing the flowers among the wild vines, the brilliant blue of the sky here, and having been under the ocean and glimpsed those wild fish, she understands that it isn't *gaudy*. She understands that here, the world is like that. Blazing with color. How could she have imagined it, back in Glendale, where from November to March there was no color at all? Where a girl walking down the street in a bright pink jacket was startling? Where a bird flitting through the gray sky with lime green tail feathers would knock the breath right out of you?

Here you wouldn't even see the girl in pink. And you would glance up at that bird, but it would be lost among the others just as brilliant.

"The temple is two thousand years old," Ander says. "Maybe older."

Incredible, Michelle thinks. Back in Glendale there was a one-room school that had been preserved as a museum. That school wasn't even two *hundred* years old, but on a field trip to it with her third-grade class it had stunned Michelle to think that the little brick house had been built so long before she'd been born. That every one of those first children who'd sat in those stiff desks in that cold room was dead.

But *two thousand* years old?

The first virgins who were sacrificed by the first priests there—could you even think of them as *dead*?

They had been gone so long that they had become something else entirely by now.

They were wind. Sky. Stars.

When Anne taps her on the shoulder, Michelle turns to look at her, opening her eyes wide, and trying to say to Anne with them, *Can you believe this?*

This is *us*.

five

Anne

MICHELLE, IN HER bright pink T-shirt and khaki shorts, looked, I thought, like an advertisement for an American girl on an exotic vacation as she stood in the parking lot next to Ander's car, stretching, holding her water bottle in one hand, smoothing her tousled hair down with the other, beaming.

Ander locked the car and began to walk toward a small open-air building with a sign over it that said VISITORS' CENTER. Michelle followed right behind him, and I hurried to catch up. When I did, I whispered to her, *"Don't you think this is weird, Michelle? Do you—?"*

But she was still smiling, and said, without turning to look at me, "Definitely! This is the best weird thing that's ever happened to us!"

A man in a white shirt sprinted over and said, "You need a guide?"

"No," Ander told him, and kept walking. Then he turned to us and said, "You girls do not need the guide. I will be the guide."

He began to walk even faster, Michelle still right behind him, but I was feeling hot and dizzy and needed a sip from my water bottle. I stopped and twisted the top off, took a long cool drink while Michelle and Ander disappeared into the Visitors' Center.

When I looked down I saw that some kind of enormous insect was crawling on its black claws through the dirt in the parking lot. I took a step back, stifling a little scream. When I looked up, the man in the white shirt was watching me with an amused look on his face.

I turned my back.

Except for him and a bus driver smoking a cigarette outside a long silver bus with VACATION EXCURSION! written on its side, there was no one in the parking lot.

But, I thought, surely, when we got past the Visitors' Center, there would be hundreds of tourists, mostly American, all around us.

Surely, Ander would not have brought us here where everyone would see us with him if he—

Anne, I thought, *you've been watching too much television.*

Anne, I heard my mother say, *don't ever go anywhere with a stranger. . . .*

six

Michelle

"CHICHÉN ITZÁ MEANS," Ander explains, *"Mouth of Heaven's Water."*

They follow him through the turnstile on the other side of the Visitors' Center.

The gravel path beneath their feet is pure white. The white of clouds. Such luminous stone, Michelle thinks, it must glow in the dark. In the middle of the night, she thinks, it must be like a shining path of moonlight.

It's still morning, but the sun is already very hot—a huge burning eye, white-gold in a pale blue sky.

On either side of the path there are low-hanging trees that make a tunnel of green over them as they walk and cast a green shade on the path's white stones. In the top branches, hundreds of birds screech and twitter and call down to them, as if trying to get their attention—red birds, small pale green ones, blue-gray birds flitting from branch to branch.

But there are also enormous black ones.

Vultures?

Ander stops and points to one. "*Zopilotes,*" he says. "They are waiting for someone to drop a sandwich or to die so they can have their dinners."

His voice, Michelle thinks, is so smooth it reminds her of the way water pours down around rocks. Everything he says sounds serious, but simple. She could listen to him for the rest of her life. She isn't, she's sure, *attracted* to him. It would be impossible to feel that way about a man so much older, the way she felt about Dave Ebert—the way the sight of his hands fiddling with the buttons on his shirt made her want to kiss the hands, unbutton the shirt.

No.

But this man, this stranger—she feels, every time he speaks, as if she's having déjà vu, again and again. As if she's known him in another life, or as if she had been born to know him again in another life. It's dangerous, she knows, feeling that she'd be perfectly willing to follow this stranger anywhere—but it's also the best feeling she's ever had, letting this man guide her into another life, or deeper into this one.

"You see," Ander says, gesturing toward the bird, "everything here is about death to feed life. The Mayans were not, as many think, bloodthirsty. They simply believed that for life to continue, there must be death. It is the same with the *zopilotes*."

Michelle looks closely at the bird. It looks back at her, staring down from a branch directly over her head. Its eyes are deep set and dark on either side of its bloodred face. It shrugs its wings, as if trying to say something—not threatening. It's simply letting her know it has seen her, and that her curiosity hasn't gone unnoticed.

Ander begins to walk again, quickly. Michelle hurries to keep up, occasionally stopping for Anne. They pass a group of tourists—about seven or eight middle-aged people, mostly couples with their arms threaded through one another's or draped casually around each other's shoulders. One couple holds, between them, the hands of a boy who looks about ten years old. He's watching something off the path, in the bush, and clearly his parents are holding his hands to keep him from going after it. If he ran off into that, Michelle thinks, they would never find him again. They're right to hold his hands.

There's a wild screaming suddenly, directly over the group of tourists, and they all startle, scatter, as their guide laughs, pointing to the treetops.

Michelle looks up to see what he's pointing at.

There, in the branches, a black monkey stares down. It bares its teeth and screeches again, and this time all the tourists, beginning to regather around their guide, laugh, relieved. They tilt their heads to watch. A few wave to the monkey, which makes an angry chattering sound, then swings away through the branches. As he does, Michelle can see his testicles—long and pink and heavy, swinging behind him.

"Jesus Christ," Anne says behind her.

Ander, who has kept walking, turns and stops then at the end of the path and says to the two of them, "Before you look, you must close your eyes. Then, when you open them again, you will find yourself to have traveled backward in time two thousand years."

Anne looks over at Michelle, as if trying to decide

whether or not to do it, but Michelle simply closes her eyes as he's told them.

"Three steps now," Ander says.

Michelle takes the steps, with her eyes closed, each one through the darkness toward the sound of Ander's voice. After the third step, she opens her eyes. And there it is:

The Temple of the Plumed Serpent.

It is the pyramid she saw on her mother's computer—but enormous.

Towering, gray and white, beneath a perfectly blue sky, in stark magnificence. All around it, the grass has been mown down to a pale green carpet, and those jagged stairs to the top look like a ladder straight to the sun, which burns brightly just behind it, like a crown.

Has she gasped?

Michelle knows that both of her hands are at her throat, and her mouth is open.

Ander smiles at her. "Yes," he says. "Here you are."

seven

Anne

ANDER LED US to the base of the pyramid—an awful dizzying ascent into a sky so pale and empty it was terrifying. I was tired, and worried, and I was angry at Michelle.

She knew better, I thought—didn't she?

Why was she so perfectly enthusiastic about following this stranger, trotting behind him as if she were his pet?

Back at home in Glendale, I knew she would never have done this. The second he started talking about *life eating death*—and those vultures staring down at us with their horrible faces—Michelle would have turned to me and either laughed crazily and nervously, or taken off running with me back to the Visitors' Center, to find a bus, to get the hell away from him. We'd have stood around gasping and panting and nearly peeing our pants. We would not have *followed* him, like a teacher or a priest or a father—as if we *knew* him.

Okay, I thought, I'd been stupid enough to get in a car with him, stupid enough to let him drive us here, but I was not going to be stupid enough to let him lead me and my friend around this creepy place then drive us back—if he even *planned* to drive us back.

The water bottle I'd brought with me was already empty, and my eyes were stinging from so much sun. I'd left my sunglasses and the other bottle of water back in his Renault, but I was never going back there to get them, because as soon as I could slow Michelle down long enough to say something, long enough to talk sense into her, we were getting away from here, from him.

We walked together to the base of the stairs and looked up.

It was like a terrible dream.

A steep ascent to the top of the pyramid, but looking, from this vantage point, like an ascent straight into the sky.

The steps were narrow, their shaded edges green with moss. There was only one guy climbing them at the moment, and one older woman coming down. They looked small and vulnerable up there. It would take only a gust of wind, I thought, or one misplaced step to send them plummeting to earth.

"It is here," Ander said, "where the Maya believed the membrane between this world and the world of Quetzalcoatl was parted. To climb these steps was to enter a place without birth or death. Most who climbed never came down again, because there"—he pointed to the crown of it—"a priest waited to cut their throats, their souls joined the Plumed Serpent, and these stairs ran red with their blood."

I took a step backward.

I tried to catch Michelle's eye, but she was looking up at the top of the pyramid, holding a hand over her forehead like a visor.

I looked too.

Up there, above the temple, a few of those black birds were circling, gliding slowly, their enormous wings outstretched—and a few other birds, bright white ones, were spiraling and spiraling just above them, as if they'd been caught in a funnel of breeze made by the *zopilotes* and couldn't break out.

"So, shall we climb?" Ander asked.

"No way," I said.

But Michelle was already seven steps up the side of the pyramid.

"Michelle!" I called after her. "It's too steep, we—"

"Are you crazy?" She looked over her shoulder at me. "Do you think you're ever going to have the chance to do this again?"

eight

Michelle

BY THE TIME Michelle reaches the top of the pyramid and turns at the temple, she's exhausted, out of breath, dizzy from the height and the heat and the exertion, and the happiest she has ever been in her life.

To climb those steps, Michelle thought as she was doing it, was to make a pilgrimage to heaven—like having decided to go to the sky, and going.

Her water bottle has been left behind with Anne, so she's thirsty. But it doesn't matter. She's also weightless, bodiless, giddy. All around her, just blue sky now, and she feels as if she could tilt her head back and drink that sky. Or spread her arms and find she's grown wings, and fly. Or slip out of her body altogether and join it—the sky, the birds, the vastness.

"Are you ready to turn around now? To look down?" Ander asks.

She is.

He's beside her, also looking up into the sky.

"You know," he says, "if you had climbed these stairs two thousand years ago, as a Mayan maiden, this would be your last moment, the last thing you would ever see."

She says, "I know."

"Then, turn around," he says.

Ander puts his hands on her shoulders and turns her.

She looks, and gasps.

It's the brightest, most dazzling thing she could ever have imagined seeing.

She can see *forever*.

She can see the whole world—miles and miles of jungle, and all of it rolling under an ocean of sky. She can see to the end of the earth. She can see the way the earth is held by nothingness in space. She can see *eternity*.

It's nothing like what she's seen from airplanes in the past. That was too far away from the world to really see it. *This* is above the world, but still *of* the world. From here she can see clearly, for the first time, *everything*. It's like the glimpse under the sea she had the day before, except that now, instead of seeing what she'd never seen before, she is seeing everything she's seen all her life—the earth she's always taken for granted—but seeing that world from the point of view of its creator. The minutest details are plainly visible, as if seen through a microscope rather than from a distance—the white stones scattered in the grass, each leaf on each tree, as if the light of the sun is pouring out of them instead of onto them. A single white butterfly catches her eye as it wobbles through the air on the horizon. And even the air itself she can see—bright with dust motes and pollen. There are two furred and golden bees in a bank of pink flowers in the direction of the Visitors' Center. She feels certain that she could count the blades of grass from here if she had time. How distinct each one is! It's as if someone—as if *God*—has gone among them and carefully folded each one. There's a rustling overhead, and she looks up. Four *zopilotes* soar in the sky above the temple, and Michelle can see not only each dark feather in their wings, but the very fibers of those feathers, the small threads of them, and the cool white bones they cover. From the talons of one, a scrap of flesh clings, damp and red.

But there are other birds, too.

Pure white ones flying in faster, smaller circles beneath the vultures.

Michelle can see the eyes of one of them—gray and calm and looking down on her.

There's also a green bird—a wild tufted thing with long tail feathers. It doesn't circle. It merely flies past, but, as it does, a single green feather falls from its wing and drifts downward, toward her. Michelle holds out her hand, and although she knows it will take a long time—that this little feather is almost as light as the air it travels through—she also feels certain that eventually it will settle in her palm if she leaves her hand open long enough and is willing to wait.

nine

Anne

THERE WAS NO way I was going to go up there. I didn't like flying, I didn't like heights, I didn't like Ander or this place, and I was wishing we'd just stayed back at the hotel, gotten drunk and met some boys, played volleyball on the beach, ended up puking in some college kid's room. Or, I wished we hadn't come to Mexico at all.

I'd put on sunblock before we left the hotel, but I could feel a kind of watery sizzling going on just under the surface of my skin. I was going to blister, peel. I felt faint. We'd spent three hours in Ander's car driving through the jungle, and had only had granola bars for breakfast. I was truly afraid that if somehow I managed to climb to the top of that pyramid, I would get dizzy, or sick, and I would never be able to get back down. I remembered my mother telling me about a woman she worked with who'd been convinced by her children to ride a donkey to the bottom of the Grand Canyon. The woman had told them she didn't want to, that she was afraid, but her children had laughed at her and insisted, and sure enough when she got down to the bottom of the Grand Canyon she'd had a panic attack and been completely unable to get back on the donkey to ride back. They'd had to send a helicopter for her.

I imagined myself at the top of the pyramid, waiting for a helicopter.

"Come on!" Michelle had said, but when she could see that it wasn't going to work, that I really wasn't going, she handed me her water bottle and said, "Well, you'd better go sit in the shade, Anne," pointing to the only tree with any shade around it for miles—a craggy spooky-looking thing at the center of the long dry lawn surrounding the pyramid.

I said, "I will."

I said, "Don't stay up there very long. I don't like this. At all."

Michelle just smiled—infuriatingly patient and

naive—and then she turned to follow Ander, who was already halfway up the pyramid.

He was wearing, still or again, that white shirt with the sleeves rolled up and khaki pants. The back of his neck, beneath the blond fringe of his hair, was brownish-red above the collar. It looked like leather, and I wondered how long Ander had lived in the tropics, and where he'd come from before this, and why I hadn't thought to ask these questions before letting him drive us here and letting my best friend follow him happily up the steps of an ancient ruin.

If, I thought, we survived this trip, and went home, and resumed the lives of ordinary American high school seniors who'd gone on spring break to a foreign country, I would never, *never* tell anyone how stupid we'd been.

I crossed the dry lawn to the tree.

The shade around it looked pale and insufficient to keep the blazing sun off my bare arms and legs, but I sat in it anyway, and put the bottles of water down next to me.

The trunk of that tree was like nothing I'd ever seen. So smooth that it would have looked like a huge human limb if it hadn't been gray. The leaves were long and shaped like feet or distended hands, and there were heavy pods hanging from the branches.

Those pods looked like an old woman's dangling breasts.

I looked at the dirt around the base of the tree, where it had grown out of the ground, and I could see where the roots had cracked into that barren-seeming soil, and those cracks seemed to go on for miles and miles under the ground, as if that tree were growing straight out of the center of the world.

Or out of hell.

I hated the tree, and those cracks into the earth around it, but what choice did I have but to sit under it and wait for Michelle and Ander to come back down and retrieve me? If I went back to the Visitors' Center they might never find me. They wouldn't know where I'd gone, and there were suddenly many more tourists around the pyramid than there had been. Busloads of new arrivals must have been dropped off, and now they were wandering across the lawn, following their guides, or stopping with their cameras, pointing them at the pyramid. Maybe Michelle wouldn't be able to track me down among them. I'd be lost in that crowd.

Or, if I left this spot, took my eyes off Michelle—who knew?

What if we were separated and I never found *her*?

So I sat down beneath the creepy tree. I took a sip from Michelle's water, which had somehow stayed cooler than mine, and which tasted sweeter. I watched her, in that pink T-shirt, walking steadily higher and higher. Ahead of her, Ander had receded, begun to look less like a man and more like a cloud in his white shirt, with that white-blond hair. And Michelle, too, blurred. A rising pink form. I thought, when she finally got to the top and turned around, I would stand up and start to wave my arms, jumping-jack style, around my head. Maybe she'd see me. Maybe she'd see it as some sort of cry for help and hurry back down—or hurry as fast as one could down steps that narrow, that steep.

Or, maybe, by the time she got to the top, she'd be scared, too.

Maybe Ander would finally have given her the creeps he gave me.

Maybe she'd have thought of some way for us to get out of there without having to ride back through the jungle with him.

I heard, then, a loud wolf whistle behind me, from the direction of the Visitors' Center, and turned around.

There were three guys walking toward me, all in T-shirts and shorts. One of the T-shirts said HOTEL DEL SOL on it, with that now-familiar rising-sun logo. One of them, a tall lanky guy in a white T-shirt, had taken the two fingers with which he'd whistled out of his mouth, and raised his hand to wave.

I waved back.

"Hey!" he called to me as he got closer. "We know you. You're one of those girls from the hotel. We know your friend Terri." (Was I mistaken? Did the one in the orange T-shirt next to him roll his eyes then?) "You're from Illinois, aren't you? So are we."

The sight of these three guys (vaguely familiar, or was I inventing that?) from Illinois was such a relief I felt like laughing out loud. I felt like throwing my arms around them, although I didn't know them at all. Their goofy Midwestern high school haircuts—one with a buzz cut and a big pirate hoop in his ear, and the other two with some kind of bad chops that gave them bristled crowns over the tops of their scalps and nothing but bare white skin in a circle from ear to ear—seemed incredibly simple, and reassuring.

They'd probably gone out and gotten haircuts for this trip, and the one with the hoop earring had gotten the piercing thinking he'd look tropical and cool in Mexico with it, hoping to look hip for the girls.

But it hadn't worked.

The boys looked beefy-faced but soft, like boys who'd been overweight in elementary school, then gotten on the football team or started cross-country but never excelled, always retaining a shadow of baby fat and awkwardness.

But I liked that about them.

Their T-shirts and shorts were reassuring, too, and the fact that one of them had been dumb enough to come out here in flip-flops and a muscle shirt. I could see that the tops of his feet and his shoulder blades had burned to a brilliant pink. Soon, that skin would blister horribly.

"I am," I said. "I'm from Glendale. My name's Anne."

"I'm Doug," the one with the white T-shirt and buzz cut said. "And this is Pete"—he pointed to the one in the muscle shirt and flip-flops—"and Robbie," he said, pointing to the one in the Hotel del Sol T-shirt and the pirate-hoop earring. "We're from Forest Hills."

"Wow," I said. "Small world."

I had no idea where Forest Hills was, but I could tell by the name that it was closer to where I lived than I was now.

"What are you doing here," Pete asked, "by yourself?"

"I'm not by myself," I said. "My friend's here. She's at the top of the pyramid."

I pointed in the direction of Michelle, who was still standing pinkly where she'd been before. It looked to me as if she had her hand outstretched, as if she were trying to catch something in it. Behind her, Ander had his hands on her shoulders.

"Yikes," Doug said. He started to rub his buzz cut self-consciously, I thought. It was hard to tell whether or not he was muscular. His arms were big, but it might have just been fat. Still, it crossed my mind that Michelle might like him. That gesture, the touching of his hair, as if it worried him, made me think she might—that bit of vulnerability on such a macho guy.

"Your friend's way up there," he said, "if that's her in the pink."

"I know," I said. "I wouldn't go. That thing scares me."

"Yeah," Pete said. "We just wanted a road trip, ya know. We wanted to see what was around here besides hotels. But this sucks."

"Yeah," Doug said. "I don't know. I thought it would be different. This is too quiet. It's creepy."

"I think so, too," I said. "When she comes down here, I want to leave."

"How'd you get here?" Doug asked.

"Well," I said, "that's the thing—"

ten

Michelle

SHE'S FORGOTTEN THAT her hand is outstretched, that she's waiting for the green feather to fall into it, but then a bit of breeze blows it away from her palm just as she remembers, and when she reaches out to grab it, she loses her balance and begins to feel herself slip into the air. Ander grabs her elbow and says, "Whoa." He plucks the feather out of the air and hands it to her.

"Thank you," she says.

She looks at it for a long time in her palm. It seems to her she has never seen anything so beautiful in her life, but also that it has always been hers. She has been carrying this feather with her, inside of her, since the day she was born.

Ander says, "It is very steep. You must be careful going down. Look at nothing but your feet on the steps. And remember that most who climbed this pyramid did not need to worry about coming back down alive. But you want to be one who does."

"Let me," she says, "just look around for a minute. Please."

"Yes," Ander says. He takes a hand off her shoulder and points to the right, to two long white walls with an expanse of green between them. "There," he says, "is the ballcourt. The captain of the team that makes the first successful shot is sacrificed to Quetzalcoatl. It is a great honor. A guarantee of entrance into heaven."

Michelle squints, and tries to imagine—the game, the players, the ancient crowds watching, cheering. A strange light shimmers over the grass.

"And there"—Ander points to her left—"is the Temple of the Warriors."

Michelle looks. It is a massive structure surrounded by hundreds of columns. The columns, lined up as if they are the warriors, continue on into the jungle as far as the eye can see, finally disappearing into it, devoured by vines and branches.

“If you look there”—Ander points beyond that jungle—“you see in the distance the *cenotes*. This is the Mouth of Heaven’s Water, for which Chichén Itzá is named. These are the sacrificial wells where Mayan maidens are taken, offered. The wells are full of such girls and their jewelry and their last songs. They are led—fifty, sixty girls on one day—in a procession along the trail through the jungle. They will be dressed in white, adorned in flowers and gold, and thrown into the wells one by one to become the brides and handmaidens of Quetzalcoatl.

“Perhaps they go willingly, joyfully. Or perhaps they are drugged, or go by force. But they never rise again, because the mud at the bottom of the wells is so thick that whatever goes into it is swallowed for eternity.”

Michelle can see them, the wells—small whorls of dark but shining water cupped by white stone and vines, flowers dipping their delicate faces into them.

She can see, too, the trails through the brush and jungle.

She can imagine the girls in their white dresses, knowing they are on the last walk they will ever take.

She listens.

She can hear them—a cool, rising ribbon of song traveling over the centuries to her. The last song of those girls. Their most beautiful song. And she can imagine singing that song. She can even imagine being willing to die for a feathered serpent, a god!

Suddenly, she sees what it is they wanted:

Something powerful, in charge of their souls, a reason to be alive, and something worth, eventually, dying for, too.

eleven

Anne

A FEW BEAUTIFUL notes suddenly spread themselves across the green lawn between the tree under which I stood with the three boys from Illinois and from the top of the pyramid where Michelle stood with Ander.

The notes were so bright and delicate that at first I thought they were coming from the sky, but then I looked up, saw Michelle, and recognized her voice instantly.

That music was Michelle.

She was *singing.*

And we weren't the only ones who'd looked up when we heard those notes, who'd stopped everything to listen. All around the pyramid, tourists were standing still, gazing in the direction of that song. When the music stopped abruptly, the last notes continued to echo and chime all around Chichén Itzá—the stones and lawn, even the tree under which we stood seemed to shiver with the echoed bits of sound and light—until they were swallowed up by the jungle, replaced by silence.

"Is that your friend?" Pete asked.

"Yes," I said, still looking in her direction.

"Jesus," he said, and looked over at his friend Doug. Both of them were sneering.

"Is she nuts?" Doug asked. He was shaking his head. The other boy, Robbie, in the Hotel del Sol T-shirt, looked equally uncomprehending. It occurred to me to say, *No, she's not nuts. She's a singer,* but it also occurred to me that I was embarrassed—of her, for her.

It had been beautiful, that song, but normal girls from Illinois high schools did not sing at the tops of pyramids in public, no matter how beautiful their voices were. I thought, then, longingly, of Terri, who would be hanging out happily on the beach by now. Wearing that bikini. Flirting with a new boy today. Maybe caught up in a game of volleyball, or having a Sky Juice at the tiki bar. I thought of the way Terri, easily and simply, would have put on some lipstick and sunblock before she left the hotel, and how just about any joke told by the right boy would make her laugh. Terri, unlike Michelle, did not fall into black moods that lasted for days. If Dave Ebert had dumped Terri, she would have laughed. Or, she would never have gotten involved with a weirdo like Dave Ebert in the first place.

Why was it that I'd attached myself so much more firmly to Michelle than to Terri, who was, in every way, a perfectly good friend? An easier friend. There she'd been all these years, perfectly willing to be my best friend, and I'd chosen Michelle instead.

Terri would never have taken this ride from Ander.

Terri would never have wanted to see ancient ruins more than the beach, the tiki bar, or a disco, in the first place.

"No," I said. "She's not nuts. But I want to get her out of here. How did you guys get here? Can you give us a ride back to the Hotel del Sol?"

Doug shrugged. "I guess so," he said. "We rented a Jeep. It's pretty small. You'll have to sit on each other's laps."

He was rubbing his head again, slowly, and didn't look very interested in taking us with him in his Jeep. It seemed strange, since these were three guys alone in Mexico at the moment, and *they'd* approached *me*. It occurred to me that maybe I looked bad—blotchy, sweaty from the drive in Ander's Renault, and from our hike here from the Visitors' Center. Maybe these guys were here hoping to find a prettier girl.

Or maybe they were wary now, of Michelle—that singing at the top of the pyramid. Maybe Doug had decided we were too weird to hang out with. And neither of the other two boys looked particularly intrigued by the idea of having our company in their Jeep back to the hotel either. Pete said to Doug, "I thought we were going to that party. At the Club Med. You know. The one close to here."

"Oh, yeah," Doug said. "Wanna go to a party first?"

This time I shrugged. "Sure," I said. "Okay. Whatever. I just want to get my friend away from this guy and—"

"He's an old dude," Robbie said. He was looking up at Michelle and Ander, who'd begun to walk down the pyramid slowly, carefully, together.

"Yeah," Pete said. "He's after some jailbait pussy."

I took a step backward, and Doug punched Pete in the shoulder. "Watch your language around the lady," he said.

Robbie snorted loudly through his nose.

Pete said, "Fuck you, man. I'm just tellin' it like it is."

I noticed for the first time that Pete had very small eyes. Eyes like a crow's. Dark, set far apart, and beady. He was a very ugly boy.

"Let me talk to her," I said.

twelve

Michelle

IT WILL NOT, Michelle thinks, be as exhilarating, as mystical, going down these steps as it had been going up.

If only there were another hundred steps rising above this one.

She'd climb them happily.

She'd climb them forever.

How wonderful it would be to look down, then.

All her life, she thinks, this is what she's been waiting for:

An adventure in the sky. A chance to see it all from a new perspective. To breathe it. To sing it. In Mr. Friedler's English class, when they'd read *The Odyssey*, she'd loved it at first. The stories, the adventures, the long winding route from Troy to home. Then, halfway through, she realized that if she had been an ancient Greek, the odyssey she would have had would have been no odyssey at all. If *she* had been a character in that epic, she'd have been sitting in her house in Ithaca, weaving something and unraveling it for ten long years. She would have been plagued by boredom. She would have simply had the task of killing time for the span of an entire life.

And it didn't help to tell herself, well, thousands of years had passed since then. That things were different now. That now, women could join the army. Girls could grow up to be astronauts. Because no woman Michelle Tompkins had ever met had ever done these things. Every woman she knew spent her days, basically, at home, or in an office—weaving and unraveling, weaving and unraveling—while men joined the army or became astronauts.

Even her mother, who'd been adventurous once, had given up her adventuring when she'd had Michelle. What choice had she had?

But now, here, Michelle is at the top of the world, looking down. She wants to go higher and higher.

She wants to stay here. Maybe not forever, but *longer.*

But she can't. She has to follow Ander down the pyramid now.

"You know," Ander says, turning to her, "at the center of this pyramid there is a passageway that leads to the altar on which the hearts of the sacrificed, still beating, were placed in offer to Quetzalcoatl. Would you like to see that?"

"Yes!" Michelle says. "Definitely."

"It is a narrow passage, and very hot, but if you are brave, we can go."

"I'm brave," she says.

thirteen

Anne

"MICHELLE," I SAID when I got close enough that she could hear me. I gestured behind me, at the three guys, with my thumb. "We—"

"Anne," Michelle said. "You should've come. You wouldn't believe it. It's— I can't even tell you. There are no words. It's—"

"Great," I said, "but, Michelle—"

"Here," she said, holding out a green feather to me. "It fell out of the sky, right into Ander's hand. It's mine, but I want you to have it."

I took the feather.

It *was* beautiful—iridescent, emerald, like a little jewel. I held it up to the sun for a moment, and then I stuffed it into my back pocket.

"Look, Michelle—" I said.

Ander came up behind her then. He nodded at me politely. In the sunlight, his blue eyes seemed to pulse with light. I looked away from him, then back at Michelle.

I said, "Can I talk to you alone? Over here?"

I gestured a few feet away from Ander, who took a step backward and held his hands up, waving them a little in front of him. "Oh, yes, of course," he said. "I will be over there—"

He pointed to a long white wall crawling with vines and moss and carved with skulls.

He bowed a little before leaving us alone.

"I'm done with him," I told Michelle when we were out of his earshot, taking a deep breath, nodding my head in his direction. "I want us to get away from Ander."

"What?" Michelle asked, narrowing her eyes at me. She looked suddenly very serious, and very surprised. "What?" She shook her head.

"We're not going anywhere else with that weirdo. He's a pervert. He's—"

"You're nuts," Michelle said, backing away from

me, shaking her head. "And we have no choice anyway, Anne. He brought us here. We can't just *walk* back to the hotel."

"We're going with these guys," I said. "I know them. They're from Illinois, and they've got a Jeep."

"No," Michelle said. She crossed her arms stubbornly. "No. You can go back with someone else if you want, but I'm going into the pyramid, into the middle of it, with Ander."

"No, you're not!" I was practically shouting now. My fists were clenched. "This has gone too far, Michelle. These guys know Ander," I said, and looked in their direction. They were standing in a line, looking at us. "They say he goes around hitting on young girls. He's looking for 'jailbait pussy,'" I said, making quotation marks in the air. "I *knew* there was something wrong with him. This is stupid, and dangerous, and now we're getting out of here."

Michelle didn't say anything after that. She just looked at me. I couldn't hold her eyes, and looked down at the grass between us.

"How do they know him?" she asked after a long silence.

"From the hotel," I said.

"These guys are staying at our hotel?" Michelle asked.

"Yeah," I said. "They know Terri."

Michelle snorted a little at that. It made my heart beat faster with anger. I felt like telling her that Terri was a hundred times saner than she was. That *Terri* was my best friend. But I said nothing. The important thing now was to get out of there, back to the Hotel del Sol, where, if I wanted to have a confrontation with Michelle, I could.

"Have they *talked* to Ander?"

"Yeah," I said. "Sure. That's how they know about him."

This was the first time I was actually lying. Before, I'd been exaggerating, but I'd believed what I said. I knew I was right about Ander. I hadn't been lying—only working as hard as I could to make Michelle understand the truth.

But now I was lying.

"Well," Michelle started, and then looked in the direction of Ander. He had his back to us. He was crouched over, looking closely at the skulls carved into the wall. When she turned back to me, her expression was, I thought, sad. "Well, he can't do anything to us in broad daylight in public, anyway. We can get a ride home with those guys if you're so set on it, but not until later. It's not even lunchtime. Tell them we'll meet them at the Visitors' Center at four o'clock."

"What if they won't wait that long?"

Michelle looked over my shoulder at them. She said, "Judging by the way that tall one in the muscle shirt is looking at you, I'd say there's no chance they won't be willing to wait that long. We'll just finish the tour with Ander, and tell him we met some friends and we're going to go back to the Hotel del Sol with them."

Michelle was right. When I went back to the boys and told them we weren't ready to leave, and asked if it was possible for them to meet us at the Visitors' Center at four o'clock, there wasn't even any hesitation. It seemed they'd talked it over among themselves while I was talking to Michelle—and maybe she was right, maybe Robbie was looking at me as if he were interested. Not that *he* interested *me* in the least, beyond a ride back to civilization. They were all ugly, I thought, looking at those boys in the sun.

Still, there was that comforting familiarity about each one of them, too—something reminiscent of boys I knew from high school, boys I'd sat next to in homeroom for four years, boys I'd gone to elementary school with—sort of big, dumb, harmless, Midwestern boys, despite the strange surroundings. It was as if God had just lifted these boys up by the scruffs of their necks during a game of HORSE in somebody's backyard in Glendale and set them down here among these ancient ruins. They looked sort of lost, but reassuring, in it. I explained the situation to them.

"Okay," Doug said.

He seemed happy, as if whatever reluctance he'd had before about giving us a ride in his small Jeep had passed, or he'd been talked out of it, or I'd misread it in the first place.

"Cool!" Pete said. "And then we'll go over to the Club Med, right? Party there for a while?"

"Okay," I said. "That'll be great."

I looked over at Michelle. She was waving me to her. Ander was standing patiently by her side. I said good-bye to the three boys, and then followed Ander and Michelle across the green lawn back to the pyramid. I tried to smile, to act as if I were now having a good time.

But when Michelle asked if I was going to go into it with them, I said no. I'd wait outside.

I did.

I sat on the steps and watched the tourists shuffle past as Michelle and Ander disappeared into the pyramid. They were gone a long time, but I wasn't as worried any longer, now that I knew we would not be alone again in the car with Ander. The people walking around the pyramid, too, seemed more familiar to me. Like people from Glendale. Women like Michelle's mom, wearing heavy socks with their Birkenstocks. Men like Mr. Bardot, wearing glasses held to their heads with straps, carrying cameras and guidebooks.

It was not, after all, that sinister.

Yes, maybe they used to sacrifice virgins at the top of the pyramid, but that was a long time ago. In two nights, I'd be back home in Glendale. The plane trip home might be bumpy, but it was only seven hours. My sunburn would heal. It was a small, safe world. I would relax. I would not, I thought, be afraid all the time, the way my mother was. I felt better. Stronger. I plucked a piece of grass and put it between my teeth. I hummed a song of my own under my breath. I waved at an old woman in a black dress who stared at me as if she were trying to see straight through me, and only when she would not look away did I stop smiling.

When they came back out, Michelle was flushed, and wide-eyed, covered in a film of perspiration, and Ander had dark-wet sweat stains under his armpits.

"Oh, Anne," Michelle said. "I—"

This time she didn't even try to stammer out a description or to tell me how much I'd missed.

We ate lunch back at the Visitors' Center. I washed my face in the women's room sink, and bought a fresh bottle of water. Ander and Michelle were so deep in conversation about Quetzalcoatl and the Mayans that they didn't seem to notice I was there.

When we'd finally finished our sandwiches and Ander seemed to have finished his story, I followed them back to the ruins, to the ballcourt, and stood a little distance away and listened to Ander tell Michelle that it was a portal to the Underworld, and about the games—how the losers had their heads cut off and displayed on a rack.

"Here," he said, and swept his arm in the direction of a long gray wall with hundreds of skulls carved on it in vertical rows, looking like heads impaled on poles, "the heads would be placed, for display, until the *zopilotes* had pecked them down to bone." When I grimaced, Ander said, "You must understand, Anne, that death to the Maya was only an end leading to a beginning."

I nodded, and he seemed satisfied, but when he turned his back I stuck my tongue out at him.

They were horrible, those carved skulls—with their empty eye sockets and their own permanent grimaces.

But Michelle *ooh*ed and *aah*ed. She stopped every time Ander pointed out some new gruesome thing, and looked at it closely, and stood still, listening to him, staring at his face as if she were in love.

Ander then took us to the sacrificial wells—a few deep watery holes in the earth, stagnant, and dark green. I felt sick, looking over the railing into one of them, and I gasped when Ander touched my arm and said, "Do not fall in, Anne. Quetzalcoatl is already rich with gold and jade and the skeletons of girls." He laughed when he saw the look on my face. "Yes, he has all the brides and handmaidens he will ever need. And you do not want to swim in these waters, or drink from them. It is said, too, if this water touches your lips, you can never truly leave the world of the Maya."

I stepped away from the railing.

He pointed out some other ruins then—walls covered with vines, crumbling in the shadow of the jungle—and when he walked off toward them, Michelle walked so close beside him it would have looked to anyone, I thought, as if he were her lover, or her father.

Maybe he *was* her father, I thought angrily. Maybe *that* explained how they could both be so interested in such disgusting things. Michelle seemed to have an endless list of questions for him, and most of them were morbid. Feathered serpent questions. Death and blood questions. And his answers were always appalling. Now and then, she'd look over at me, smiling, as if trying to get me to lighten up. But I had no intention of lightening up.

Finally, I looked at my watch and said, "It's time for us to meet our ride at the Visitors' Center, Michelle."

"So quickly?" Ander looked surprised. "Oh, there is so much more to see!"

"Well, maybe we'll come back," I said. "But we really have to meet our friends now or they'll be worried."

Michelle shook her head at me, maybe she rolled her eyes, and went on with her questions to Ander for a bit longer, but finally she said good-bye when I took her wrist and started to lead her away.

"I'll look for you," she said to Ander, "back at the hotel, okay? I want to write down the names of some of the books you told me about."

Ander assured her he'd see her there.

"Good-bye, girls. Go safely into your next adventures," he said politely, and bowed a little as we walked away.

three

one

Michelle

THE PASSAGE INTO the pyramid had been narrow, and the walls were damp, sweaty.

"It is a pyramid within the pyramid," Ander told her.

That dampness was either humidity that had risen and condensed on the stone, or the sweat of all the tourists who'd pressed themselves through the passage in the dark on their way to the altar at the center of it.

But it felt to Michelle like blood.

Thick, and warm.

At first, she'd pulled her hand away from it quickly, but then she'd become curious and begun to trail her hand along the walls until her fingers were slimy with it. When she pulled them away again, to look, it was too dark to see what color that dampness was on her fingertips.

At one point, she and Ander and the other tourists had to squeeze sideways through the darkness. At that point an older American woman behind them said, simply, "No," to the man she was with, and turned around to leave. Luckily there was no one behind the woman, or she wouldn't have been able to go—she'd have had to be pushed through to the end.

Although Michelle herself wasn't claustrophobic, she could imagine how someone else might be, how someone like Anne, for instance, might panic in this little hot, damp space, be unable to go on, and have to go on anyway. It would be a bit like being born—unwillingly, as an adult, fully conscious, being pushed through that tunnel—except, at the end of it, there would not be freedom, but instead an altar on which the beating hearts of the sacrificial victims had once been placed.

Michelle kept her eyes closed for a few minutes, letting herself just breathe.

It was too dark anyway to see.

She was breathing, she knew, the breath of the strangers around her, and they were all breathing the exhaled air of those who'd come before them. She thought back to the top of the pyramid so she would feel less cramped. She imagined a bird beating its wings over the pyramid. She saw the two wings, green ones, flapping and flapping through the air. And then she imagined how free that flying would be if there were nothing but wings. If the heavy body of the bird were gone, and there was just flying. At the top of that pyramid, she'd been able to imagine it:

Wings without the body of a bird to weigh them down.

A rose, unfolding, with no stem.

The soul, released from the heavy, fluid-filled balloon of the body.

There it goes—she pictured it, the soul, released in a puff of feathers and green brilliance—*too light for this world.*

She opened her eyes to peek, and it was so dark, and so small—the walls in the center of the pyramid growing closer as she went farther into it—that she had to close her eyes tight again.

Still, she felt comforted by Ander ahead of her.

She could hear his steady breathing.

Occasionally he'd say something reassuring. *"Only eleven more feet. Only seven more feet."* He'd been here before, so he could tell her, because he knew.

Then, they reached the foot of a set of stairs together, and began to climb. Ander counted out the stairs for her.

One. That's it. Two. That's right.

Michelle kept her hand on his elbow so she wouldn't stumble, and then they spilled out together into an open space. Light, suddenly, was pouring down on them from some opening overhead—and there it was:

A man's face, turned, looking directly at her.

He was reclining, backward, his knees bent.

On his stomach, he held a platter.

"Here," Ander said, "is the *chac mul*, where the beating heart is offered."

two

Anne

I SAT ON Michelle's lap in the back of the Jeep because the Jeep had bucket seats. The windows were made of plastic, and as we sped down the dirt roads on the way to the Club Med party, that plastic rattled.

It reminded me of the sound my grandmother's bedsheets used to make, flapping in the breeze in her backyard. She had a dryer, of course, but liked the smell of the sun on her sheets, and I thought of her—Grandma Pam—with her pouffy white cloud of hair and her apron pockets full of clothespins, to keep myself from feeling carsick and from thinking about Robbie, sitting beside me and Michelle in the backseat. He had his hand precariously close to my shoulder, draped over the seat. I was hoping I hadn't somehow given him the wrong impression. If I had, I was hoping to have an opportunity to set it right before we got to the Club Med. The boys had said we wouldn't stay long. But I was worried that once we got to the party, Robbie would think he was pairing off with me.

Michelle, I could tell, was going to be no help.

She was off, still, in some dreamy Mayan world with Ander—staring out the window with a little half smile. She was sitting on my lap, but felt weightless to me.

It was getting dark by the time we arrived. The hotel's sign was lit up outside: CLUB MED UXMAL. Instead of the ocean, which was the backdrop to the Hotel del Sol, this hotel backed right up to the jungle. It was smaller than the Hotel del Sol, but emanating from it was the same background noise of shouts and rap music, the howling murmur of students on spring break, the occasional piercing shriek or booming laugh. Michelle and I stumbled out of the cramped backseat and followed the boys through the lounge (like our hotel, full of half-dressed teenagers and college students—some spread out on the wicker furniture, some standing, leaning against pillars, drinking from bottles or plastic cups, or kissing) and into an elevator that smelled like stale beer and vomit.

We got off on the sixth floor to a sea of partiers and a wall of music.

As I feared, Robbie took my elbow right away and began to steer me through the crowd. I looked behind us and saw that Michelle, still with that dreamy detachment, was walking between Doug and Pete—too slowly, it seemed, for Pete, who gave her a little push.

The rooms all along the corridors were open, and in most of them there was just more crowd. Naked, sunburned male backs. Girls in bikinis. Occasionally, someone jumping on a bed. Someone lying (passed out?) on the floor. But in one of the rooms I caught a glimpse of a naked girl spread-eagled on one of the beds. Three or four boys were standing at the foot of the bed, just looking at her. I hesitated. Was that really what I was seeing?

I looked more closely.

Yes.

Was she passed out, or displaying herself for

those boys?—one of whom saw me looking at him and gave me the finger. I looked away quickly and kept walking, but Robbie knew I'd hesitated at that doorway. "You want a look or something?" he shouted over the music into my ear.

"No," I said, wanting to say more:

That, if that girl was passed out, something should be done, and if anything happened with those boys, it would be rape. And where were her friends?

But he pushed me a little with his elbow toward a keg at the end of the corridor, then reached over me and took two plastic cups for us and filled them, handing the first full one to me.

Doug reached past him, and soon we were all five holding foamy plastic cups.

"Cheers!" Robbie shouted, and held his up.

Michelle and I raised our cups, too, and after Robbie took a sip, he put his arm around me. Within a second, however, there was a surging of the crowd in the corridor, and a guy with a bath towel around his shoulders slammed into Pete and knocked him over. There were screams coming from some room, and then what seemed to be ten or twenty naked girls running, followed by maybe thirty guys groping at them, trying, it seemed, to catch the girls as they ran past.

But the girls were slick, greased up—oil, lotion, soap?—and the guys couldn't hold on to them.

There were hoots, and more guys pushed through the crowd to go after the girls.

I put my beer down and looked for Michelle.

I couldn't see her anywhere.

"I'm leaving," I said, and handed Robbie my plastic cup. I started to push through the crowd, forcing my way, because I had to, and someone said, "Hey, don't shove me, bitch," and someone else elbowed me hard in the breast as I passed.

I found Michelle standing against the wall with a shocked, wide-awake look on her face. Finally, she'd been snapped out of her Chichén Itzá bliss, and I felt relieved and guilty at the same time.

It had been me who'd gotten us here.

"Let's go," I said.

Michelle followed, and we held hands, making our way back to the elevator. This time, the door to the room where the naked girl had been sprawled on the bed was closed.

"Jesus," Michelle said when we got to the elevator doors. "What are we going to do, Anne? How are we going to get back now?"

"I don't know," I snapped.

"Hey!"

I turned around. Doug and Robbie were standing right behind us.

"What?" Doug said. "You were just gonna leave without us?"

"No," I said, trying to sound apologetic—it wasn't their fault that the party was so out of control, and we still needed a ride back to our hotel—at the same time the elevator doors opened. The four of us stepped in.

"Whoa," Doug said when the sound of the corridor was sufficiently shut out to speak in a normal tone of voice. "That was some weird shit."

Robbie looked drunk already, or stoned. He was leaning against the wall of the elevator, his jaw hanging open, his eyes red. We were all sweaty, but he was dripping with it.

"Yeah," I said. "We're not staying. Will you just give us a ride to the Hotel del Sol?"

"Anne," Michelle said, shaking her head as if trying to get me to stop talking, "we can get a cab or something, I'm sure."

"Right," Doug said sarcastically, "that'll cost you like five hundred dollars. Don't worry. We'll drive you girls back to the hotel. Won't we, Robbie?"

Doug punched Robbie in the shoulder then, and he seemed to wake up a little. "Where's Pete?" he asked, looking around. "This whole thing was his idea, anyway, right?"

Doug rolled his eyes at us, then snapped his head in Robbie's direction. The doors opened, and Doug said, "Pete's coming. Let's just give him a minute."

Michelle and I followed Doug out of the elevator.

"Wait here a sec," he said. "I'll pull up the Jeep. Pete should be back by then."

three

Michelle

THE PASSAGEWAY LEAVING the *chac mul* at the center of the pyramid was carved with spotted, angry animals.

Mostly they were just faces, but a few of them were dancing, or wielding knives. Two seemed to be mating beneath a tree.

"The jaguar," Ander said. "They are the animal of the night. Of the Underworld. You see, we are now passing through the Underworld in order to be reborn."

After the light that had shone on the *chac mul,* the darkness leading out of it seemed even more disorienting. When she blinked her eyes, Michelle saw it again—that reclining man, with a basin resting on his torso, where a beating heart would have been placed.

She saw him bathed in that light.

It hadn't scared her.

She'd stepped over to it and caressed it, even run her fingers through the basin before the tourists behind her had stepped forward and nudged her gently out of the way.

"You have touched life, and death, and history today," Ander said as they walked away.

Again, the passageway seemed to narrow as they pushed through it. And the walls were cool and damp. This time Ander was behind her, and occasionally he would reach out and touch her shoulder. She knew it was just so he'd know she was there.

"You are so brave and adventurous," he said. "You remind me of my youngest daughter."

"Thank you," Michelle said.

"And what is the name of your father?" he asked.

They were almost to the end of the passageway. Michelle could see pure blue light at the end of it, and the fresh air just outside.

"I don't know," Michelle said.

Ander said nothing else until they stepped out into the world. Then he said, "See? It is easy. You have died and been reborn. Quetzalcoatl is your father after all."

four
Anne

DOUG PULLED UP in the Jeep, and Michelle and I got in. Robbie waited on the steps of the hotel for Pete.

This time I sat in the backseat, and Michelle took the front. She would move back to sit on my lap again, she said, when the other two boys got there.

When Doug got out to ask Robbie if he'd seen Pete, Michelle turned to look at me. She said, "I know you don't like him, but tomorrow I'm going to look for Ander as soon as we wake up. I had the most amazing day with him, Anne. This might not be how you want to spend your spring break, but I'm going back to the ruins if he'll take me. I'm not going to stay at that hotel and get trashed and hang out in hallways with people doing things like they were doing here."

I was tired, and the tone of her voice—condescending, impatient, serene—suddenly infuriated me. I thought of Terri, who was probably getting ready right now, back at the Hotel del Sol, to go out dancing. Putting on mascara and setting out to find some cute boys and a few margaritas seemed very appealing to me. I wanted to toss a beach ball around in the pool tomorrow with some college boy, not look at altars where the beating hearts of sacrificed virgins had been placed. I couldn't help it. I said, "Fuck you, Michelle. I could have had a perfectly nice day if it wasn't for you and your pretentious archaeological bullshit, and making a fool of yourself singing at the top of the pyramid, and following this weirdo around like his little dog. I knew we shouldn't have come. And now, if you're in love with the old guy, I say go ahead. I guess if he rapes and kills you it won't matter, since you both enjoy sacrifices so much."

Michelle closed her mouth.

I couldn't stop.

I was hot, and thirsty. I was exhausted. And scared. I said, "So is that it? You're in love with this old geezer?"

"No," she said, practically whispering.

"Well, what is it then?"

She turned away from me. I thought I heard her say, under her breath, *He's my father.*

"Jesus, Michelle," I said. I was shaking my head hard enough that I could feel the beads of sweat under my hair dislodge and begin to roll coolly down my back. Why was I so angry? I realized that I was digging into my own knees with my fingernails, and I said back, also under my breath, maybe not loud enough for her to hear, *You don't have a father.*

Doug and Robbie and Pete came out of the hotel then, and stood at the entrance to it arguing. Robbie had two water bottles in his hands, and Pete tried to grab one away from him. They were close enough that I could hear Robbie say, as he grabbed it back, "Fuck you, man. Fuck you. This was your idea."

Pete took a threatening step toward him and said, "I'm gonna kick your ass, you—"

Doug stepped between them and held up his hands. "Come on, Pete. Cut it out. Robbie, just get in the fucking Jeep, man."

Robbie started toward the Jeep, stumbled on the curb, but managed to open the passenger-side door. When he saw Michelle there he said, "Excuse me," politely, and handed her the water bottle, then walked around the other side and got in.

Beside me, I could smell the beer and marijuana on him. He was so hot and sweaty that even the plastic windows seemed to condense with it once he was in the Jeep. He looked at me and shrugged. He said, "I thought we were going to party—"

I looked past him, toward Pete and Doug. On the sidewalk near Pete's feet I saw what looked, at first, like an index finger. But then it twitched its tail, and I saw that it was a lizard.

Pete just turned around and went back into the hotel.

Doug turned around, heading back to the Jeep.

Before he did, he stepped on the lizard.

five

Michelle

MICHELLE SEES DOUG step on the lizard.

It looks, to her, as if he's done it on purpose.

In her throat, there's still something soft and damp that had risen into it when she heard Anne whisper under her breath, *You don't have a father*. If not for that, she would say something, she thinks, to Doug, about the lizard, when he gets behind the wheel of the Jeep and starts it up. She's done it before—confronted boys about such behavior. Pulling the wings off dragonflies. Kicking over anthills just to kick them. Only a few months before, she had been in a car full of kids on the way to a movie, and the boy driving had sped up when a squirrel hesitated on the road in front of them.

He'd hit it on purpose, and laughed when he did.

All the girls screamed, and Anne had even started to cry, but Michelle had just leaned up to him and said in his ear, "You asshole."

The boy went very quiet then, and turned very red.

But Michelle doesn't know Doug, and after the things Anne said, Michelle can hardly swallow, let alone speak. She and Anne have had fights before, and she knows that Anne is tired, disoriented, sweaty, thirsty. Still, something hot and dark seems to have descended—a bad curtain between the front seat and the back.

Doug pulls out of the hotel parking lot, and drives the Jeep fast through the pitch black.

Michelle closes her eyes.

She tries to go back, in her mind, to the top of the pyramid—standing there, looking down on the world—and Ander's warm hands on her shoulders the only thing that kept her from flying into the sky.

"It's so blue," she'd said to him.

"Yes," he'd said. "In the Mayan language, there are nine words for *blue*."

six

Anne

DOUG DROVE THE Jeep fast through the dark. It was impossible to tell where we were going—no signs, no landmarks, not even any painted stripes down the middle of the road. But, I thought, getting across the Yucatán Peninsula with Ander had seemed simple enough. I remembered the map—an expanse of green surrounded by blue, and only one or two dots that were towns in the center of it. It had seemed there was only one road through the jungle between Cancún and the ruins, so as long as we didn't break down, I thought, there could be no problems. We would be back in the wild pink glow of the Hotel del Sol within an hour or two. If we could find Terri, we could sit around the pool together, drinking piña coladas. Maybe Michelle would sulk back to the hotel room, or go looking for Ander. But I wouldn't care. It would give me a chance to tell Terri about the trip. About Ander, the morbid ruins, Michelle singing at the top of the pyramid. Terri would be appalled by that. "Jesus. Has she gone nuts?" Terri would say. Terri, I realized fully now, had been poised for years beside me, ready to step in to the slot of best friend as soon as I was done with Michelle.

Still, riding behind her, looking at the soft dark tangle of Michelle's hair, I'd already started to soften.

I hoped she hadn't heard me, the comment about having no father. I remembered how, when we were in second grade, a boy on the playground had thrown a snowball, which had hit me hard in the ear. I'd burst out crying, and Michelle, who'd been playing on the swings at least twenty feet away, had come running. After I showed her my ear, she wiped the tears off my face with her red wool mittens, then kissed the ear. It had, actually, felt completely better afterward.

Now, Michelle was staring out the plastic window of the Jeep at the darkness.

I closed my eyes and listened to the plastic rattling of the windows. Maybe I fell asleep. By the time I opened my eyes again, hours could have passed, or no time at all. Because nothing had changed, it was impossible to know whether we'd traveled a few feet or many miles. It was all still darkness and vegetation out there, and around us just the sound of wind and plastic and the Jeep's engine. Then Robbie said, "I've gotta take a piss."

It was the first anyone had spoken since he'd opened the door, seen Michelle there, and said, "Excuse me." And apparently the radio didn't work, or at least Doug hadn't bothered to turn it on. We had traveled in silence from the very beginning.

"Shit," Doug said. But he slowed down, and started pulling over to the side of the road. When he did, I could taste dust and gravel, kicked up by the Jeep's wheels. When he'd come to a stop, Robbie jumped out, and Doug turned to look at us, rolling his eyes. We could hear Robbie urinating—a noisy stream of it hitting the dirt. When he got back to the open car door, he was still zipping up his pants.

"Hey, that's rude," Doug said, looking at Robbie's open fly.

"Yeah, whatever," Robbie said, slipping back into the seat beside me.

Doug started the Jeep again. He reached down on the floor near Michelle's feet, picked up a water bottle, and handed it back to me. I took it. I'd been so thirsty so much of the day that I'd begun to get used to it. I almost didn't even feel the need for a drink—which I imagined was a dangerous thing and had to do with dehydration. It might have been, I thought, one of the factual warnings my mother had given me at some point. I knew for sure that she had told me that a person begins to feel very warm and comfortable just before freezing to death.

AGUA PURA the bottle said on the label—a drawing of a mountain on it, and a stream of white pouring down from its snowy peak.

"You girls can share this one," he said, "if you're thirsty."

"Thanks," I said, and took the bottle. "Do you want some first?" I asked Michelle, and handed it to her. It was my peace offering. Riding behind her, in the dark, in that silence, I had begun to miss her. She was only two feet away from me, but it felt like hundreds of miles. I wanted to reach out and touch her shoulder. I was hoping that, by the time we got back to the hotel, maybe we would be on speaking terms again. I would tell her I was sorry, that I'd just been exhausted, stressed out. If she wanted to talk about the Mayan ruins and how beautiful they'd been, I would, I thought, let her.

"Yes," she said, and reached over her shoulder for it. "Thank you."

She unscrewed the top and took a long drink from it as Doug pulled back onto the road and sped again into the darkness.

Michelle passed it back to me, but as she did, she shook her head. "Don't," she said under her breath, handing it to me, looking at me seriously. I could see the light of the dashboard reflected in her eyes.

"Don't what?" Doug asked.

He looked at Michelle with an annoyed expression before turning back to the black windshield in front of him.

"Nothing," Michelle said, but she was looking at the bottle so that I could see that she meant *this, don't.* When I tried to take the bottle from her hand she held on to it, only letting it leave her hand after she seemed sure she'd managed to look directly into my eyes, and shaken her head again.

"Don't what?" Robbie asked this time. He was also looking at the bottle of water.

Michelle said nothing. She turned around again, so I could see only the back of her head.

I looked at the bottle.

Robbie was looking at it, too.

I wasn't as thirsty as I had been anymore, anyway. Still, I held it to my lips as if I were drinking because Robbie was watching, seeming to be waiting for me to drink.

I took the smallest sip.

The water tasted, I thought, maybe a little bitter, but nothing unusual.

I put the cap on it again and put it back on the floor of the car near my feet.

We continued through the darkness on the road, which, like the one from the airport to the Hotel del Sol, was so soft and quiet under the tires that it seemed as if it had been poured only a few days earlier. Or only recently melted, and solidified again. Doug began chatting with Michelle politely. Where was she going to college next year? What did she plan to major in? What did her parents do?

Michelle's answers were quiet, and the rattling of the plastic in the windows made it hard for me to hear her. I heard Doug tell her that he was from Chicago, which surprised me. He'd said, back at the ruins, that he was from a suburb called Forest Hills, hadn't he?

After a while, they quit talking altogether, and Michelle was looking out the window again at the darkness. Robbie picked up the water bottle at my feet and handed it to me. He said, "You should drink some more. You'll get dehydrated."

Again, I pretended to take a sip, then put it back on the floor near my feet, and we drove in silence for a long time, until Robbie leaned up between Michelle's shoulder and Doug's and said, "So, was that you singing at the top of the pyramid?"

Michelle turned to look at him, and again I could see the side of her face in the lights from the dashboard. There was a trickle of sweat zigzagging down her cheek, which startled me. It was no longer hot in the Jeep. The breeze had cooled, and the humidity had seemed to lift it away from us. "Yes," she said, sounding groggy.

"That was some fucking weird thing," Robbie said.

Michelle just looked at him with no change in her expression, but her eyes seemed to close, then bat open again. She turned back around, put her elbow against the armrest between herself and Doug, then rested her head against her hand.

Robbie shrugged.

He looked over at me.

"So, is your friend a nutcase?" he asked.

"No," I said. "Are you?"

His eyes focused on me then in a way they hadn't before, as if he were truly seeing me for the first time, and didn't like what he saw. "Yeah," he said.

Michelle turned around then, as if she were going to say something, but then turned back again and seemed to sink lower in her seat.

No one said anything for several minutes. There was no sound except the darkness parting around the Jeep. Its engine. The rustling of leaves and breeze in the distance. A few night sounds that must have been jungle birds and animals: screeching, a whistle, *ahoo-ahoo-ahoo, crrrrrik*. The tires passing over tar. There were no headlights coming in our direction, and when I turned to look behind us, I saw that there was nothing there but darkness either. Robbie leaned up and said to Doug, "Pull over here."

Doug nodded.

He started to shift gears, slow down, pull onto the side of the road—the rising of dust around us, the smell of it in my nostrils—dry and mildewy at the same time.

I said, "Why are we stopping?"

I felt that I could have choked on that dust in my throat and my sudden new fear, but everything was happening too fast. I swallowed it. I inhaled. I looked around me wildly—but for what? I'd already seen that there was nothing but darkness and the four of us in that Jeep on the entire face of the earth.

"*This* is why," Robbie said, grabbing the back of my neck and yanking me toward him.

"No!" I shouted. Robbie laughed, and somehow I elbowed him hard, catching him completely in the ribs, and his hand slipped from my neck as he doubled over, shouting, "Shit. Fuck. You bitch."

I unfastened my seat belt—an afterthought, just as it had been when I'd fastened it—which gave Robbie time to recover and to grab my hair. I yanked away from him and heard it rip in his hands. It was the sound of a comb tearing through my damp tangles as a little girl, my mother saying, *"I'm sorry, Anne, but we have to do this. . . ."*

"Goddamn it," Doug said from the front seat, and turned the engine off. As the dashboard went dark, I saw that Michelle was completely slumped over in the passenger seat. Her chin was resting on her chest.

"Michelle!" I screamed, but she didn't move.

Robbie slammed my head hard against the back of her seat, and when he did, Michelle seemed to slip away altogether, held in place only by her seat belt.

I turned then and began to claw in the direction of his face. It was too dark to see what I was clawing at, but I must have managed to find his eyes with my fingernails before finding his ear, his earring, his stupid pirate hoop, yanking. *"Uh, uh, God."* Now, he was coughing, sputtering, choking. He kicked me away from him, and when he did I fell backward against the plastic tarp over the Jeep windows and fell through it, onto my back, into the dust, into the darkness, still screaming for Michelle. It was like having been born a second time, into the world, alone.

I got to my knees and tried to grab the passenger-side door handle, but when I did, Doug started the Jeep up again, and it sped away in a seething gust of gravel, with no headlights, and with Michelle still buckled into her seat.

seven

Michelle

SHE KNEW AS soon as she tasted it on the back of her throat that there was something wrong with the water. But she was so thirsty. It was as if her body had taken over in its need for water and would not let her take the bottle from her lips, forced her to keep drinking, to swallow.

She had felt a thirst like this before. At the drinking fountain in the hallway at school after gym class, twelve laps around the track on a hot September afternoon. There might have been seven kids behind her in that line, four of them boys who were jostling each other, saying, "Come on, Tompkins. You gonna drink all the water?"

But she was too thirsty to stop. It was cool, and

flowing, and her body needed it, and if at that moment someone had tried to pull her away from the fountain, she would have held on with both hands to try to fight it.

And she remembered being a little girl, too, in the wading pool at the Holiday Inn where she'd stayed overnight with her mother while they were visiting cousins in Bloomington.

She'd cupped some of that water in her palms (was it really aqua-blue, or was that the color the pool was painted?) and drank it.

"Michelle!" her mother had said, standing up fast from the lawn chair in which she'd been reclining. "Don't drink that! It's dirty!"

But it hadn't tasted dirty.

It had tasted sweet, and soft, not at all like the water that came out of their tap back home in Glendale.

When her mother turned her back again, to smooth her towel out beneath her on that lawn chair, Michelle did it again. She couldn't help it. In her mouth, that water tasted the way she imagined morning glories would taste if the petals could be melted down and left to cool. Dazzling, and completely satisfying, as if everything else she'd ever had to drink—7-Up, Hawaiian Punch, orange juice—had all been a pale imitation of this.

But the water in this bottle hadn't been like that.

It had tasted like ordinary water, but bitter—something chemical lingering under the purity of its plainness. It had been her thirst that had made her drink it. Not the wild desire that had overcome her at the drinking fountain. Not the curiosity she'd felt at the pool.

It had been, simply, physical.

Plain, ordinary thirst.

When the darkness begins to slip over her, she knows exactly what has happened, and why.

She turns to look at Anne, but Anne is gone.

four

one

Anne

HE'D NEVER TURNED the lights back on, so I had to chase the sound of it—running and screaming, "Michelle! Michelle! Get out of the car!"

I ran after the sound of the Jeep's motor, the sound of its wheels rushing over the road, the vague angry grunts of Robbie in the backseat, the rattling flap of the plastic on the windows. I ran faster than I'd ever run before in my life, but completely blind. I thought, crazily, that maybe I was running so fast that I could reach out toward the sound and grab the bumper of that Jeep.

Somehow, I thought, if I could just run a bit faster, I could grab the bumper of it, and pull that Jeep to a stop. I could—

But it was pitch black all around me, and the sounds of the Jeep grew more distant. I tried to run and listen at the same time, but I could no longer hear the engine.

Still, I kept running, and my running and my hearing became, I thought, superhuman. I could hear the sound of Michelle's steady breathing as she sat slumped in the passenger seat. I could hear the sound of her hair moving around her in the wind through the broken window. The sound of her eyelashes fluttering. The little click of her swallowing. I heard all of these things as I was running, and ran after those sounds until I could hear nothing at all, and then I dropped to my knees in the road, in the darkness, and put my face in my hands.

Nothing.

How far had I run?

How long?

The tar of the road was warm.

On every side, I was surrounded by nothing.

It was all gone, having sped so fast and so far ahead of me that it was now as though I'd imagined it completely.

It had never been close enough to touch at all.

"Michelle," I said into my hands.

For what must have been a long time, I stayed where I was, like that, kneeling in the middle of the road, in the middle of the jungle, waiting for the pounding of my heart to grow quieter so I could take my hands away from my ears, so I could swallow, and breathe again, and stand up.

When I finally did, I staggered.

It was impossibly dark.

No moon. No lights.

I put my hand out, as if the darkness itself could steady me, or to feel it. To see if there was something, someone, anything, nearby.

But there wasn't.

Overhead, the stars were a mass of light, but it was smeared and dim and disorienting. I couldn't see by it. Except for a bit of shimmering on the leaves of the trees at the side of the road, those stars lit up nothing.

And then the sounds of the jungle began.

Of course, they'd been there all along, but over the pounding of my heart, and my screams, I hadn't been able to hear them yet.

Now, I could.

Cackling. Rustling. Hissing. Murmuring. Things thrashing through the brush. Crawling along the ground. Beating their wings through the air. Landing on branches. Swinging through branches.

I heard a heavy huff, an exhalation, and turned quickly in the direction of it, my hand over my mouth to try to keep myself from screaming—but of course I could see nothing.

But I *had* heard it.

And I heard it again, and stepped backward—but where could I go?

I was standing in the middle of a narrow road surrounded by jungle. There was nothing but more narrow road ahead of me, forever, and behind me, for miles—what good would it do to begin walking in either direction? I knew the Hotel del Sol had to be at least sixty miles away. Eighty. We'd been in the Jeep for an hour since the Club Med, at least, driving seventy or eighty miles an hour. How long would it take for me to walk back? All night? Or longer? And what good would it do me to retreat into the jungle? Whatever kind of animal was breathing from one direction, it would have its equivalent on the other side of the road—or it would simply follow me there.

I sank back to my knees, put my hands to my ears again.

It was impossible, I thought. It wasn't happening. It *hadn't* happened. It was a dream.

It was a dream that had formed itself around some terrible kernel of truth. Something I'd read. Something I'd been warned about. Something my mother had said could happen if I didn't wear sunblock, if I walked alone at night, if I believed everything I heard, if I took a ride with a stranger.

But *this* could not be happening.

Those boys, they'd been too familiar. They'd been from our home state. They'd known our friend. Everything about them—what they wore, how they spoke—it was as ordinary to me as anything I saw on any particular day at Glendale High.

No.

I had not traveled to Mexico, to another country, to a foreign place full of strange ruins and lizards and a language I couldn't speak to be kidnapped and drugged by boys from home.

No.

Michelle had not been taken away by them. She was not slumped in their Jeep. She was not going to be raped, or killed, or abandoned, as I had been, in the jungle.

No.

I was not crouched alone in the middle of a road in the middle of a jungle in a foreign country, thousands of miles from home.

No.

We had never left the hotel. We were drinking Sky Juice at the edge of a pool that had been cleaned and chlorinated. We were waiting for Terri. We were going to the disco. We were laughing about what could have happened if we'd—

No—

We had never even come to Mexico for spring break!

We were at home.

When morning arrived, we would go to the mall. We would check the movie listings in the paper. We would go to a movie. It would be like this:

Something terrible happening to two girls on spring break. Midwestern girls. Girls like us.

But, unlike us, they'd made a mistake, and something terrible had happened.

And then the movie would end.

And the lights would come back on.

And we'd stroll through the lobby together afterward.

It had been a matinee.

It would still be light outside when we stepped out of the theater.

It had never been this dark.

I would never know how dark it could be on a road, alone, in the middle of a jungle, far from home.

I had started to believe it—there on my knees on the black tar of a road laid down through jungle in the middle of the Yucatán Peninsula.

I had nearly calmed down enough to stand, to begin my slow waking, my gradual walk away from this dream and back into the world, where the thing that seemed to be happening to me had never happened, *could* never happen—and then I heard something—breeze, motion, breathing—traveling toward me on what sounded like wings beating, or wheels, whistling over tar. I leaped to my feet and whirled around to face it, and what I saw made me scream.

The scream was enormous.

It caused rustling in branches, and what sounded like panicked running through the jungle. I put my hand over my mouth to stifle it, and looked closer.

What *was* it?

Something traveling toward me at great speed—a darkness inside another darkness, this one with arms and a head—a hat, could it be wearing a hat?—and wildly moving legs, a hundred times faster than any human legs could move. And the legs made a whirring sound. Wings. Scissoring wings. Some kind of hovercraft? Some bird-snake-animal I'd never heard of? Something supernatural? It was flying over the ground. It was shearing through the air straight at me. It was shouting over my screaming with a man's voice. *Could it be?* Was it shouting in words, in Spanish—shouting so loudly and with such panic that it sounded as if it, too, were screaming, terrified, beside itself with terror, shouting itself hoarse with terror but still flying wildly in my direction with those wings glinting in the starlight sending sparks in every direction with its feathers, shouting the whole time, until it screeched to a halt, panting, a few feet away from me—and I saw that it had not been *flying.*

It had been pedaling.

In the dim starlight I saw that it was an old man in a straw hat who had been riding a bicycle, and that the look on his face reflected the terror I felt.

two

Michelle

AT FIRST, SHE thinks the breeze is singing. It's too dark to see even a few inches ahead of her, so she simply closes her eyes to listen to it:

The chiming of small, glass bells?

Are the bells strung from the branches of trees?

Or are they floating in the air?

Is the breeze scattering them so that they fly into one another and make this light, crystalline music?

Tiny bits of broken vase and champagne flutes?

Shattered, with voices?

No.

She opens her eyes slowly, letting the darkness pour into them until she thinks she can open them all the way and not be drowned and blinded by it.

Her eyes begin to adjust to the darkness, and when they do she sees that, in the sky overhead—miles and miles into that dark vastness, far past where the clouds would be if there were clouds—there are birds.

Thousands of them.

Millions.

Silver-and-green-winged. Singing. Lit from within, it seems, so that she can see that the brilliant music she'd heard was striking off their wings in sparks—their feathers exploding and falling away from them, dissolving in the darkness, turning into those bright notes.

She opens her mouth, and the breeze seems to blow over her tongue, into her throat, and for the first time, she inhales, and realizes that she is alive.

Had she thought she was dead?

No.

She'd thought that she'd not yet been born.

She closes her eyes again.

three

Anne

"NO, NO, NO," he stammered, shaking his head.

Was he telling me not to scream, or was he trying to convince himself he wasn't seeing what he was seeing in the middle of this dark road through the jungle?

Was he also dreaming?

He put a hand to his chest, caught his breath, began to speak softly to me in Spanish.

"No, no, por favor. Por favor. Chica—"

I couldn't understand what he was saying, but the musical hush of it convinced me to close my mouth, to stop my screams, to sink back down to my knees in the road.

He held out his hands, then, as if to show me that

they were empty. He got off his bike, set it carefully down on the ground, and took one slow step toward me. He asked me a question, and his voice was still soft, and low, but I couldn't answer the question. I didn't know what he was asking, and I was sobbing. But his voice was full of compassion, kindness. It was the crackling voice of a very old man. It was hard to see him clearly in the dark, but when he got closer I looked up and through my tears could see that he was very skinny and that his hands, still held out in front of him, were shaking.

He asked me a question again, and again I shook my head. I said, "I don't speak Spanish. No *español*."

"Oh," he said. "Oh."

And then he sank to his knees, too, about three feet away from me.

I could hear his knees pop when he did—a simple, painful sound.

His face, when it was closer to mine so I could really see it, looked terribly old. Ancient. There were more wrinkles around his eyes than I had ever seen, as if he'd spent centuries and centuries squinting into an unbearably bright sun. The eyes themselves were dark, watery, but they searched my face with nothing other than curiosity, I thought, and concern. He was looking at me closely and with as much astonishment as I was looking at him, trying to see me in the gray starlight. He smelled, I thought, like strong coffee, and with that scent came a clear and painful memory of my mother, only a few days before, standing in the kitchen with an open bag of coffee beans, pouring them into the grinder.

I started to heave then with sobs, and to cough.

The old man put a hand on my shoulder and said something that sounded sad and reassuring, and then he took his hand from my shoulder and folded his hands in his lap, and just stayed there on his knees, looking at me.

We stayed like that, facing each other on the dark road, for what seemed like hours, or weeks.

Months. *Centuries.*

After I stopped crying, we sat in silence.

Occasionally, the old man cleared his throat.

After a while he got off his knees and sat down cross-legged.

A few times, he opened his mouth as if he might say something, and then thought better of it, or remembered that I wouldn't understand him anyway, and so said nothing.

But after a while, I felt infinite comfort in his presence, in his throat-clearing, the sound of his breathing.

I felt as if I'd known this old man all my life. As if he'd come to me through the darkness on his bicycle just for this purpose, to watch me through the night.

He didn't have to tell me why he was staying with me.

He was staying with me to keep me safe, or to keep me company, at least, until the sun came up.

He must have thought about it, finding me there, and realized it was the only thing he could do.

Or someone, something, had sent him here to do it.

And the sun did eventually come up.

In inches, at first.

Just a bit of light filtered through the brush on the horizon, looking like a cool, pink stain spreading. And then like light. And then like a fire starting somewhere far away.

As it grew lighter I could see him better. His skin

was a deep reddish brown, his lips spotted, but his teeth were bright and white, and, in the sun coming up, I could see that his eyes weren't as dark as I'd thought they were. There were flecks of gold in them, really. Although his face was as wrinkled in the sunlight as it had been by starlight, the eyes set in that face were much brighter and younger than I'd thought they were. He had the most beautiful face I'd ever seen, or would ever see again, I knew.

When it was light enough, he stood up and went to his bicycle. He said something to me again in Spanish, got back on his bicycle, headed in the direction from which he'd come, wobbling at first, and then riding away from me very fast.

I watched him pedal away until he was only a shadow, and then a mirage, and then a memory, and then the sun rose high enough in the sky that I knew it was morning.

That the night was over.

The dark had been so complete that it hadn't seemed possible that in such a short time the sun could be pouring down on everything—every leaf and bird, on my arms, on the black road (which began to grow even softer under my shoes), and the dust at the side of it—and bringing so much color to it. I stepped off the road, into the shade. A few small emerald lizards scurried away when I did.

I stood like that, at the side of the road, in the emerald light, listening to the birds—thousands of them, it seemed, just waking up in the branches—and trying to breathe slowly, and not to cry.

It was morning. Daylight. The old man had gone, I felt sure, for help. I was thirsty, and my head pounded from the crying and the terror, but I tried not to think about where I was, where Michelle was. I trusted the old man. He would have taken me with him on his bicycle, I knew, if he had not had a plan that would be swifter, better—

And then I heard the sound of tires.

A car, this time, traveling over that softening tar.

I stepped out of the shade and into the sunlight, holding my hand over my eyes so I could see it. It was still just an emerging shape in the distance, but I recognized it immediately. Ander's Renault. I stepped into the road, waving my hands over my head, shouting, "Please! Please!" as it sped closer.

four

Michelle

WHEN SHE OPENS her eyes again, it's daylight. She's alone in a jungle lying on her side with her knees pressed into her stomach, her arms wrapped around her legs, her head tucked into her chest. When she unfolds herself and lies back and looks around her, she's stunned to see how beautiful it is. *Creation.* So much whispering green, and, above it, a color there is no word for, for which a word would have to be invented.

five

Anne

ANDER WANTED TO turn around, to go to the police in Mérida near the ruins and the Club Med where the boys had taken us, but I said no, that we had to go in the direction they'd gone when they left, that Michelle might have been dumped along the way, or she might have escaped. She could be anywhere now. She could be wandering along this road ahead of us, or at the side of the road, and that I had to be able to look. The one thing I knew was that the boys had not turned around and driven back down this road. They had taken Michelle and they'd kept going.

So he agreed to go back to Cancún along that road. "Yes," he said. "Perhaps we will see her. Perhaps—"

We drove in silence for miles, and I kept my eyes on the side of the road.

Could she be out there, somewhere?

Had she, like me, spent the night in the jungle, on this road in the dark?

Had they kicked her out of the car, or had they pulled over again, and she'd regained consciousness, escaped?

Had the Jeep broken down?

Maybe they'd left it, with Michelle in the passenger seat. Maybe they'd never intended to do her any harm. Maybe it had been *me*. Because of Robbie. Maybe they'd simply opened the car door and let her go, and she was wandering now, looking for *me*.

It seemed possible, and the only hope, in this expanse of green and bush, that maybe Michelle was on this road, and that we would find her if we kept looking. After a while, my eyes burned with the dust and sun, but I was afraid to blink, afraid to miss her. Ander seemed to be doing the same thing—scanning the sides of the road, looking out the windows and into the mirrors, but driving very quickly at the same time.

I wept, but without closing my eyes, wiping the

tears away as quickly as I could, so I could see her. I thought of what I'd said to her: *I guess if he rapes and kills you it won't matter, since you both enjoy sacrifices so much.*

It had *all been* because of *me.*

She had trusted him, and I had trusted *them.*

Ander put his hand on my shoulder, and we drove like that until the ocean could be seen ahead of us in all of its turquoise glory, and the frothing of waves on that white sand, and the road cluttered with beautiful students in bathing suits, holding paper cups, glistening with sunblock and sweat.

Seeing them, like that—the hordes of them, in their ignorance, their drunkenness, their youth, their oblivion, their joy—took my breath away.

six

Michelle

BLUE?

No.

There would need to be a better word.

Where is she?

Who is she?

She sits up.

She puts her hands to her face and feels it. And then the hair on her head. She looks at her hands:

Are they hers?

If they are not hers, whose are they?

She uses the hands to push herself up from the ground. To stand.

She uses the hands to brush the dirt off her knees, to rub her eyes. She is naked, but she isn't cold. The air around her is soft and damp, and the sun overhead pours onto the leaves around her, and their soft green light seems to clothe her.

She's surrounded by vegetation. Trees strung with heavy vines. Bushes with flowers on them—red and blue, white, pink. She can't see anything in any direction except overhead, because wherever the wall of green opens, another wall of green waits behind it. Except for herself and the green around her, and that *blue* overhead, there is nothing. Empty. Not a sound. Nothing singing. Nothing breathing. Nothing. She blinks, then opens her eyes wider and looks around.

seven

Anne

IN ANOTHER MONTH, when I am back at Glendale High for my third and last day, I will overhear two boys I've never spoken to (juniors, in letter jackets, whose faces are bulldoggish and unmemorable) talking to each other in the hallway:

"You know what they did to her, don't you?"

"Sure." A chuckle.

"Yeah, well, that. Anybody would do that, you know—some drunk girl in the fucking jungle. Sure. But then they dragged her out there, you know, where there's nothing, and they burned her to ashes."

"Yeah? What makes you so sure?"

"How else could you hide a body so good? I mean, the cops and the FBI and her mother and every newspaper writer in the world's been out there scouring every inch of that place. She's ashes, man. She's not even ashes. She's on the breeze, man. She's on the bottom of some poor fucker's shoes."

They laughed.

I was standing—a statue, struck dumb—behind them.

The books I was carrying I dropped at my feet.

I put a hand over my mouth, and then Terri was behind me, *What? What? Anne? What?* And then Mr. Bardot was running toward me down the hallway with his arms outstretched, a pale panic on his face, and tears in his own eyes. Terri stepped out of the way, and Mr. Bardot grabbed me hard enough to make me stumble backward, and then he put his arms around me and pressed my face to his chest with his hands. "Oh, Anne," he said. "Oh, Anne."

I didn't cry. I stayed like that, in the dark polyester smell of Mr. Bardot's chest for a long time. The bell rang, and the hall was emptied, and when I looked up, the boys were gone. In Ms. Gillingham's office, which smelled of candles and dust from an old velvet shawl she wore around her shoulders, the assistant principal called my mother.

"It might have been the wrong idea," Ms. Gillingham said, "to insist that Anne come back to school. This is just too hard. She can finish her work at home, and graduate in plenty of time."

"Yes," my mother said. "Oh, dear, yes."

Back at home, my mother made me a grilled cheese sandwich, and brought it to me on the couch, where I sat looking at Michelle's senior portrait lit up on CNN—that perfect, strained smile.

She hated having her senior picture taken, and she'd hated this particular picture most of all.

"I look like a zombie," she'd said.

Now, the whole world it seemed had been looking at that picture on their televisions for a month—Michelle, electrically bright, distilled into a million little bits of glitter and shimmering, her eyes too wide, her skin airbrushed by Ralph's Portrait & Passport down to a soft and lifeless ivory.

She looked, even *I* thought, like someone to whom something terrible would happen.

But we all did, didn't we?

Any one of our senior portraits could have given that impression—blown up, backlit.

"Maybe you shouldn't watch that," my mother said. "Anne, if there's any news, we'll hear it before it's on the television."

But she knew that wasn't true.

We'd gotten nothing special, nothing earlier than anyone else except for one phone call from Michelle's mother, who was still with Ander in Cancún—who'd called to tell us that, in a small jungle village deep at the center of the Yucatán Peninsula, they'd met an old woman who said she'd heard of a young white girl who did not speak Spanish who'd been found wandering at the side of a road, but the old woman could not say where the girl had been taken.

They'd arrested one boy, but let him go after I was sent the photo—I'd never seen this boy with his red hair and freckles in my life—and his alibi (a disco in Cancún) was confirmed. Since then, there'd been no more arrests. Not one person on the Yucatán Peninsula who remembered a Jeep and American boys. No boys who matched their descriptions from any of the thousands of American towns named Forest Hills. And so many boys who matched their descriptions from every other town that it was impossible to find any of them at all.

No one called to tell us about the tennis shoe they'd found in the brush off the road between Chichén Itzá and the Hotel del Sol—which had not, in the end, been Michelle's—although for hours on the news they'd implied that it was, the serious jaw of the anchorwoman telling the world that this shoe meant that Michelle Tompkins, the high school senior from Glendale, Illinois, who'd disappeared during her spring break in Mexico, was as good as dead.

And then there was the strand of hair found in a rental car that had been returned the day after Michelle's kidnapping (not a Jeep, and which had not been rented to American boys but to a Danish couple on their honeymoon), on which tests were still being run.

The police in Mérida had found, finally, the old man on the bicycle who'd stayed with me through the night. He'd never seen the second girl that night in the jungle. He'd found Ander at a rooming house where he'd spent the night. Ander was the one person the old man knew in his village that night with a car, and he never saw another vehicle that night or morning on the road. Until the police questioned him, the old man said he'd thought that he might have dreamed the whole thing.

There was a girl from the Club Med who vaguely remembered seeing someone who looked like Michelle in the hallway, but even under hypnosis she couldn't describe the boys who'd been with her or remember anything that might lead the police to them. And there was a girl who'd been staying at a hotel down the beach from the Hotel del Sol, who told police that she, too, had been drugged by some boys who said they were from Illinois. She'd woken up naked on the beach. She couldn't remember anything. She hadn't wanted to tell anyone what had happened until now.

I could not turn away from the television.

At any moment, that senior portrait might come to life:

Michelle, in her pink shirt and khaki shorts, wandering out of the jungle—sweaty, bruised, but smiling.

What could I do but watch?

eight

Michelle

ALL OF CREATION is spread out before her.

She has no idea which way to go.

nine
Anne

I HAD REFUSED to get on the plane back to Illinois with Terri, although the police had said there was nothing I could do, that I had given them all the information they could use, that they would call if there was anything else they needed to know. Ander had said it was dangerous for me to stay, because I was so tired, and he would be searching, himself, and he would not be able to look out for me. When Michelle's mother arrived on the next flight to Cancún, he and the police would need to be working with her. But I had put out my hands and said, "No. How can I leave?"

On the phone, my mother begged me, and when she realized I wasn't going to come home with Terri, she booked her own flight to Cancún.

* * *

I'd still believed, then, that we would find her within hours, and then, within days.

I believed, then, that yes, something terrible had happened. Yes, she'd been drugged, she'd been raped. But they had let her out of the Jeep, and then she had gotten lost. Soon, Ander, or the police, or the FBI on their way from Washington and Chicago to the Yucatán Peninsula, would, with special tracking devices—helicopters? dogs?—find her.

She would need to stay in the hospital for days, maybe weeks, because of the dehydration, and for special tests—pregnancy, AIDS, neurological damage. Back home, she would need counseling, because of the trauma, because of the rape. Maybe, instead of college next year, she would stay back in Glendale until she was feeling stronger. I would stay, too. We would go for long walks, when she wanted to. She would have nightmares, and call me in the middle of the night. I would rush over with bagels. Little by little, she would get stronger. I would help her get stronger. I would devote my life to it. She would stop having nightmares. We would pick out a dog, together, at the animal shelter. It would give her strength. Eventually, she would find a gentle boyfriend. I would be a bridesmaid in her wedding. We would hold each other after the ceremony, and weep. *Thank god, thank god, you have come this far, you have survived.*

Right after our drive through the jungle, after we reached the ocean without having glimpsed her, and gone to the police, where Ander spoke to five young men in blue uniforms in rapid Spanish, I had begun to believe that, no, she was not in the jungle after all.

They had brought her to the Hotel del Sol. She was in our room. Maybe she had not even been raped. Maybe the boys had found Terri, who helped Michelle to bed, where she was now. Maybe they hadn't meant to drug her. Maybe—

But the policemen looked over their shoulders at me, and I realized then that there were streaks of dirt up and down my arms, and I could smell the sweat on myself.

At one point, one of the uniformed men nodded in my direction, and then asked Ander something. Ander turned to me and said, "Anne, the officer wants to know if you are okay? Do you need medical care?"

The policemen all looked away from me then when I shook my head, and I realized suddenly that they thought I had been raped.

I looked like a girl who had been raped.

And, for the first time, it occurred to me that this is what they'd planned. Those boys. They'd planned to drug us, and to rape us, and to kill us, perhaps, and I'd escaped, and Michelle had been driven away into the darkness, and a little scream floated from my mouth, like the ghost of a scream, which I could actually see—white and tissuey and shaped like a bell—hovering in the air in front of my face, before everything slid away, and I felt my head slam against the floor.

When I opened my eyes again, Terri was the first thing I saw.

She was sunburned, wearing a white tank top, her hair a wild mess around her face, although it looked as though she'd tried to pull it back into a ponytail. And I could smell something—rum? tequila?—on her breath. It took me a few seconds to understand where we were.

We were in our room at the Hotel del Sol.

I recognized my own bikini, strung up on the back of the chair. The sliding glass doors to the balcony were open, and I could hear screaming laughter coming from somewhere beyond the crash of waves and wind.

And then I remembered why I was there, and realized how I must have gotten there, and what had happened, and I sat up fast and screamed, "Where is she? Where's Michelle?"

"Oh, god," Terri said, grabbing my head and pressing it to her chest. I could smell her sweat and the sun on her, and the sea—salt, sky, sand. "Oh, Jesus," she said. "Nobody knows. The police went off with that Ander guy, to look for her. Oh, Anne, what happened? What *happened*?"

Terri started to wail. She put her head in her hands, and I could see that the skin on the back of her arms had begun to peel. Under the red, there was a painful-looking dampness, which was new skin. At some point she had forgotten, after all, to wear sunblock.

I got out of the bed, and Terri looked up at me. She said, "Ander said not to go anywhere. Not to let you get out of bed until—"

I picked up the phone. It was the worst thing I could imagine doing, and the only thing I could do. What else?

When my mother answered, she sounded so close I imagined I could have touched her. I imagined I could smell her perfume. She was at work, eating lunch at her desk, and she sounded breezy, peaceful. *Hello?*

On the line between us were all those thousands of miles—I could feel those miles, suddenly, in the air, spinning out ahead of me. I could see them, as if from the sky. The billions of steps between us. The long, blistering walks through deserts, the dark nights through forests, crossing mountain ranges, our hands bleeding, to get to each other—the lakes we'd have to cross, the rivers full of salmon, slippery stones. We would have to walk through blizzards, and windstorms, the farmers waving to us from their porches, and the animals—cows, coyotes—watching us with their blank stares, and the birds circling overhead, the tropical birds, and the dull gray birds, and the *zopilotes.*

To be this close to my mother again, I knew, I

would have to travel a lifetime, and at the end of it I would be a completely different person.

I would have become, by then, the girl on the other end of the phone who said to her mother the words she'd dreaded for as long as she'd been my mother:

"Mama, something terrible has happened."

ten

Michelle

THEY COME FROM every direction then, wearing feathers, their faces painted with white and yellow stripes. They carry spears. They speak a language she doesn't understand. Two of them lunge for her and pull her up by the arms. She hadn't even realized that she'd fallen to her knees. She starts to scream, and then one of them strikes her with something—his hand? the spear?—on the side of her head, and everything falls away in a brilliant flash.

After a while, she stops screaming, and she no longer tries to pull herself away from the two who have her by the arms. There are too many of them. She doesn't even need to walk. When she slows down, they just lift her again, as if she weighs nothing, as if she is a rag doll, so that her feet drift over the dirt and she doesn't even need to move them. They don't speak, but she can hear them breathe. The serious inhalations and exhalations that sound like just more rustling in the jungle, which has pressed in on them as the dirt road narrows into a footpath.

For a long time, there is silence. Occasionally, the screech of a bird. Now and then one of them clears his throat. Far ahead, at the end of the path, she thinks she can hear a rumble of thunder, or drums. But mostly just her heartbeat. In her ears, and everywhere around her. Perhaps she's bitten her tongue. She thinks she can taste blood in her mouth. She can smell the oppressive perfume of flowers floating out of the jungle, and the sweat of the men surrounding her, and herself—her flesh, her hair. She closes her eyes.

eleven
Anne

BY SEPTEMBER, THE senior portrait of Michelle had been replaced by a blurry snapshot of a journalist who had been kidnapped in Baghdad.

By October, it was the school picture of a boy in Alabama who had strolled through a supermarket with an Uzi, killing people he'd never even met.

In November, there were car bombings, a woman who'd thrown her baby out of the window of her high-rise in Boston, a Chinese immigrant family who had been on a day trip to an amusement park and were hit head-on by a semi.

There were scandals involving money, politicians, spies. There were mudslides in California. An earthquake in Chile. A flood. A hurricane. A supermodel who'd overdosed. A businessman who murdered his girlfriend. A bank robbery that went wrong, and everyone in the bank was killed.

I didn't go to college.

My father stopped trying to talk to me. He would kiss me on the head when he came home from work, but then he would go into the den.

I ate my meals in the living room, in front of the television.

Michelle's mother did not come back from Mexico. My own mother went to check on their house, their cats, and to bring in their mail, which was delivered now only once a week in four or five enormous bags—all letters of condolence, or paranoid rantings, or prayer cards, rosary beads, psychic predictions from people who knew about Michelle, each envelope already sliced open by the FBI agents assigned to open every letter addressed to Michelle Tompkins or her mother.

Occasionally, Michelle's picture would flash across the screen again.

Always the same smile.

The caption under it the same—

Missing Girl.

twelve

Michelle

OH, HE IS *not a human. He is a god. His feathers rustle around her as he takes her by the shoulders—but his skin is also the skin of a snake. Cool, daggered, iridescent. When the knife is raised, she isn't afraid. She does not close her eyes. After the first plunge into her chest, she feels nothing more. Not fear. Not sadness. After the next, he reaches in, and what he pulls out is the most luminous blue-green bird she has ever seen. It is newborn, but it has always been alive, and he lets it fly from his hand into the sky. She watches it crashing into the blue, singing beautiful notes, a few of its green feathers falling from its wings, settling quietly around her.*

Go, he says, releasing her.

She looks down and sees that there is nothing

there, where the bird has been pulled out. No scar. No blood.

But she also knows that what he's taken from her is everything she was.

She turns.

It takes her a long time to walk back down the steps, but she knows it will do no good to look back.

When she reaches the bottom, she keeps walking, because she knows it no longer matters where she goes.

She walks, naked, into the jungle.

She walks without stopping.

She walks for all of eternity without any idea of where she is going, or where she has been.

thirteen

Anne

MY FRIENDS CAME to say good-bye when they left for school, and hello when they came home for weekend breaks. Terri brought me a framed picture. She'd taken it the first day of spring break, when Michelle and I had emerged, sunburned, from the ocean. In it, we were glistening with salt, squinting into the sun, our arms thrown around each other.

Still children, I thought, looking at it, and then turning it over, flat, on my lap.

"Was it wrong for me to give this to you?" Terri asked.

"No," I said. But after she left, I put it in a dresser drawer, piled T-shirts and sweaters on top of it, and closed the drawer.

* * *

In December, Christmas came and went. My mother put up a tree. She took it down. She brought magazines home from the drugstore with her. *Vogue. Elle. Self.* Before she gave them to me, she went through them and weeded out the ones with stories about Michelle. At night, when I woke up screaming, she came into my room and lay down next to me. Once, in frustration, because I wouldn't eat some tomato soup she'd put in a coffee cup for me, she said, weeping, "I thank god every day that it wasn't you, Anne, but it might as well have been you! You never came back either!"

Then, on New Year's Eve, the phone rang. I was in bed already, staring up at the dark ceiling. I could hear through the walls that my mother was excited. Her hushed, quick questions. I sat up in bed, fast. I was just swinging my feet onto the floor when she rushed in with the phone. She said, "It's Michelle's mother."

I must not have moved.

In the light from the hallway, my mother's face glowed as if someone had taken a snapshot of her with a bright flashbulb.

"We've found her," Michelle's mother said on the other end of the phone.

"Oh my god," I said.

"Here," she said. "Say hello to her, Anne." I could hear Michelle's mother saying, *It's Anne. Michelle. Say hello to Anne.*

"Hello? Hello? Michelle?" I was shouting. I was screaming. My mother put her hand on my shoulder. I said more quietly, *"Michelle? Michelle?"*

On the other end of the line, I heard nothing.

We turned the television in the living room up loud enough that we could hear the reports upstairs as we dashed around tossing toothbrushes and socks into suitcases.

The missing Glendale girl has been found. After a ten-month-long massive search by FBI and international detectives failed, the tantalizing rumors that had spread since the girl's disappearance have proven to be true: that, in a small Yucatán village, a white girl was living who fit the description of the missing girl. Michelle Tompkins was found this morning in good health in the remote village of Tuxaptlehuac, in which fewer than one hundred people live and which is isolated by jungle, cut off from all paved roads. At this report, the missing girl is with her mother in a hospital in Mérida, Mexico.

My father was on business in Chicago. My mother called him, and sobbed into the phone. "They've found Michelle." Before I zipped up my suitcase, I remembered the green feather, the one Michelle had given me when she came down from the top of the pyramid with Ander. I had found it in the back pocket of the shorts I'd been wearing—later, back in Glendale, unpacking the soiled, sad clothes from spring break—and I'd kept it on a bookshelf near my bed. Now I took it down and put it in a large envelope next to the framed picture of Michelle and me blinking into the sun on the beach outside the Hotel del Sol.

There we were:

Two girls on spring break, wearing new bathing suits, glistening with water and salt, arms tossed around each other, in a faraway land, a million years ago.

I zipped the suitcase closed.

My mother locked the front door behind us.

Her hands shook as she started the car, and as she

drove she held the steering wheel so tightly that her knuckles went from white to pale blue. We listened to the radio. Occasionally, we would look at each other—in awe, and fear. At a stoplight, my mother put her hand to her mouth, and a stifled scream came out. Merging onto the freeway, I sobbed—once, twice—and then I stopped. On the airplane, beside her, I kept my eyes open as we hurtled down the runway. I wasn't afraid of flying this time, but my teeth were chattering. When the flight attendant asked us if we would like a beverage, we both stared up at her as if she had spoken to us in a foreign language. Neither of us spoke. The flight attendant repeated the question, and my mother looked at me, and we both began to laugh. *She had been found! She had been found! She was in a hospital. Her mother was with her. She hadn't spoken, but it didn't matter. She was alive. It was impossible, and it was the only possible thing in the world.* Everything else was inconceivable, questionable, unlikely—history, butterflies, the combustion engine, the Dewey decimal system—but the fact that Michelle Tompkins, the Glendale girl who had disappeared ten months before, had been found alive in a little village in the Yucatán Peninsula and was recovering in a hospital in Mérida, Mexico—this had always been the most probable thing in the world.

We held each other's hands.

Now and then, my mother would put her arm around me, pull me to her, and instead of crying, we laughed.

We landed at sunrise.

At the airport, two FBI detectives picked us up in a black car.

The sun was pink and orange in the sky.

The world, it seemed, had been created for this.

"She seems to be still in shock," one of the men said grimly, looking at us in the rearview mirror, where we sat with our arms around each other, smiling.

"Yes," my mother said. "But she's been found."

"Yes," the other detective said. "But she's not, it seems, quite who she was when she was lost."

"We know," I said.

We did know.

The radio in the car on the way to the airport had said as much, had said that, although the missing girl from Glendale appeared healthy, she seemed to be suffering from complete amnesia. It could be because of the trauma, it could be because of the drugs, or perhaps some sort of head injury had been sustained. She responded when she was spoken to with blinks, and even, once, a smile, but she didn't speak, and she didn't seem to recognize anyone, even her mother, or know where or who she was.

This is not unusual, an expert was quoted as saying, in cases like this. *Yes, it could be due to a head injury, or the drugs, but more likely this is a reaction to trauma. No one has any idea what this girl has been through. It will take some time to determine what her condition is, and what the chances for her complete recovery are. But the important thing is, she has been found, alive.*

fourteen
Michelle

SHE'D SEEN JAGUAR'S eyes—luminous gold disks in the night.

She'd heard their grunts, their roars.

She'd seen fireflies lighting up whole groves of trees. Monkeys who spoke an ancient dialect to one another. A macaw that turned into a man, and then into a tree. She spent many nights under a thatched roof, she ate, and then she wandered away, following the sound of a bird in the jungle.

It was singing a familiar song. She was trying to hear that song because it reminded her of someone she'd known once. Someone who had flown away. Or someone she had been. Long ago, it seemed, she had lost track of the bird, the song, and had wandered, knowing nothing, hearing nothing. Occasionally, a thought drifted across her mind, but it was gone before she knew what it was. Kind people brought her soup. Their cats slept curled up with her on blankets on the ground at night. They moved their hands around their faces, seeming to ask her questions—but of course she couldn't answer. She had no answers. She wandered for centuries. Her feet grew calluses and her skin grew dark. She learned which fruit could be eaten, and which made her sick. She used her teeth to tear the meat off certain plants. She drank from moving streams. She came upon a colossal head made of stone. For a long time, she looked at the head, and it looked at her.

They'd known each other, she felt certain, when they were alive.

fifteen

Anne

WHEN I SAW her there in the hospital bed—not asleep, but not awake either—staring at the ceiling, I took three steps toward her, and then I sank to my knees.

"Anne," her mother said, turning to me.

She was holding Ander's hand.

She looked from him to me.

"Oh, god," I said.

I could say nothing else.

I couldn't stand.

The floor of the hospital room was made of red tile, and it was cold and painful on my knees.

The girl in the bed looked at me curiously then, blinking from the ceiling to me.

"Anne," my mother said, "it's Michelle."

My mother went, then, to the bedside and took the girl's hand, and began to stroke it.

"Anne," my mother said, looking from the girl to me.

But I could only watch from the place where I knelt on the hospital room floor.

Ander said, in his soft and flowing voice, "She will know you again, although she does not know you now."

Michelle's mother made a small, sad sound in her throat, and Ander put his arms around her, and pulled her to him.

I stayed where I was, on my knees, unable to stand or to speak, while my mother stroked the girl's hand, whispering to her. Next to the girl's bed, a window was open, and I could hear the riotous music of tropical birds outside. The sun shone through the blinds onto her face. She looked from my mother to me with her large, blank, blue eyes. She had never seen me before, I could tell, and, although the eyes were the same shape, and the hair was the same color, and the face was Michelle's face, and I recognized the opal on her right hand, and even the pink sheen of her fingernails, and the shape of her lips, and the length and curve of her neck—I'd never seen this girl before in my life.

We never unpacked or checked in to a hotel. Instead, by the end of the day, the FBI had arranged for a private jet to fly us back to Illinois. New clothes had been bought for the girl, and after she was dressed in them—a sleeveless pink top, a green skirt, flat white shoes, and a white sweater—her mother snipped the tags.

The girl put out her hand, for the tags it seemed, and her mother gave them to her.

She looked at them closely before letting them slip from her fingers onto the floor.

As we left the hospital, nurses and attendants came out from behind their desks to watch us walk down the corridor—the girl, her mother, Ander, my mother, the two detectives, and me.

They were completely quiet in their white uniforms, seeming to be holding their breath, as if watching a solemn parade of ghosts pass by.

* * *

Through the spring, she spent her days on her mother's back porch, looking out at that flat emerald square of the backyard. Sometimes, the shadow of a bird flying from a branch to the feeder seemed to intrigue her, and she would stand, take a few steps toward the sliding screen door, and look more closely, but then she would sit down again, fold her hands on her lap, and resume the quiet blinking.

She ate whatever her mother put in front of her, in small, silent bites. If Ander (whose tan faded in Illinois, whose hair grew darker, and who, in April, married Michelle's mother in a private ceremony at the courthouse while my own mother and I stayed with Michelle) put a book in front of her, she would page through it carefully, but quickly, as if looking for something in particular. Not finding it, she would close the book and give it back to him without saying anything.

She was taken to her psychiatrist on Mondays, her physical therapist on Tuesdays. On Wednesdays, art therapy. On Thursdays, my mother and I would spend the afternoon and evening with her, to give Ander and Michelle's mother a break.

At first, I visited her every day, and then, only on

those Thursdays, and only because my mother had made the commitment. My job at the library kept me too busy to go every day, I said.

But of course that wasn't it. It was her stare, and the stranger's face she had returned from the jungle wearing—the one that bore such a strong resemblance to the face of my friend, but wasn't hers.

In the summer, her mother took her for walks. A television show came and did a story about her. And then another. And *Newsweek, The Atlantic, The New Yorker.* They always asked to speak with me, to take my photograph, but after the first one I refused.

In the fall, I signed up for classes at the community college.

At Christmas, my mother gave her a beautiful Mexican shawl.

Ander helped Michelle's mother wrap it around her shoulders, but while we sat at the dining room table, opening the little presents we'd gotten for one another, the shawl slipped off her narrow shoulders onto the floor, and it stayed there.

She never noticed.

* * *

Then, at the end of February, a guidance counselor from Glendale High called me and asked, apologizing at the same time she was asking, if I felt enough time had passed since what had happened that I might consider coming to the school and speaking to the students and their parents about spring break.

There were, of course, a number of students who would be traveling to Mexico, the Bahamas, Aruba, Bermuda, for spring break, and she thought I might have some things to say that might be meaningful, that might help them avoid, as she called it, "having something terrible happen."

No, I said, and hung up.

But a few hours later I called back, and said yes.

I wrote down the details of what I would say on note cards. I wore a black skirt and a white blouse. I started the talk with, "You've all heard by now what happened to Michelle Tompkins on spring break." I tried not to look up. There were maybe a hundred people in the auditorium. I said, "I brought this photograph of us, the day before it happened, to show you. We were in Cancún. We'd gone snorkeling. It was our first day of the trip."

I slid the framed picture out of the manila folder in which I'd slipped it the year before, when I'd packed it for the trip to Mérida, the day Michelle was found.

As I did, with my hands clammy and shaking and those hundreds of eyes on me, the photograph slid out of that envelope, the green feather also slid out, and it wafted to the floor at my feet.

sixteen

Michelle

SHE TRAVELS FOR centuries through a dark tunnel. Now and then, the shadow of a bird flashes across her face, and she startles, looks up, but it is never the bird—the one with the blue-green feathers, the one that was pulled from her chest and flew into the sky, the one she lost.

It is always a dull gray bird. Or something flecked. Something brown. A bird with pearl-colored feathers.

There are pages to turn, and never that bird.

There are faces, looking into her face.

And all the time she is traveling, traveling, by foot, or crawling, or only in her mind, and even in her sleep, through that dark passage at the center of the temple.

They bring food, and place it before her, and she eats.

They bring her blunt scissors and construction paper, and she cuts the paper, pastes one piece to another.

They play music for her, place shawls around her shoulders, blankets on her lap.

And then, again, that quick flit of a bird, and she looks up.

And then, she is in the passageway again.

The blue light at the end of it always receding. Always in the distance. She is walking. She is crawling. She is moving through a million years of blood and feathers toward that light.

And then—a flustering of wings, a song.

But it is never the song.

It is never the feather.

And then, one day, the girl with red hair kneels at her chair.

She has tears on her face.

She opens her hand, and, in it—

seventeen

Anne

I SPOKE QUICKLY after that, maybe too quickly for the audience to understand what I was saying, holding that feather the whole time, afraid to let go of it. They asked me questions in serious voices, and I answered as quickly as I could. When someone's mother stood up and said, "Thank you, Anne, for being so brave, for coming here tonight to speak to our children," and they all began to clap, I said *thank you, thank you*, and gathered my things and ran out to the street to the curb where I'd parked my mother's car, got in it, and sped as quickly as I could to Michelle's house. Without even ringing the doorbell, I burst in, hurried to where she sat at the kitchen table, and knelt down with the feather in my palm, holding it out to her.

eighteen
Michelle

SHE LOOKS AT it and says, “Oh,” taking it from the girl’s hand, “Anne.”

And Anne says, “Michelle, Michelle—tell me, where have you been?”